Chris,

Hope you
enjoy the
book!

Mary
Kok :)

A

GREY

RESORT

WENDY M. KOK

ISBN: 978-1-54397-049-4 (print)
ISBN: 978-1-54397-050-0 (ebook)

For Mom, Dad, and Trish

CONTENTS

"There will be signs in the sun, moon and stars. On the earth, nations will be in anguish and perplexity at the roaring and tossing of the sea. People will faint from terror, apprehensive of what is coming on the world, for the heavenly bodies will be shaken."
Luke 21:25-26

PROLOGUE

*M*y first real experience of knowing "things" occurred was when I was five years old. The day will be etched in my brain always. It was just another ordinary summer day, and I was riding along with my dad in his favorite car. It was a Corvette, and the color was fire engine red. Dad loved that car and always seemed to take good care of it. Often I saw him in the driveway polishing it up in the sunlight.

Dad and I were buddies that day, running errands together in our small town. I was stuck in the passenger side because the gear shift took over most of the front seat. Although the Corvette was important to my dad, I had conflicting feelings about it. I never told him that I hated riding in that car. I always felt uncomfortable and fidgety sitting in my seat. There was no good reason for this, other than I always felt like something terrible was waiting for us while riding in it.

Which, in the grand scheme of things, it wouldn't be that hard to imagine. It was a sports car and dad liked to drive fast. The odds of getting in an accident were pretty good. So, here I was, leaning against the window on the passenger side. Without a care in the world and hoping we would make a little pit stop to Dairy Queen to get a Peanut Buster Parfait.

But instead of ice cream, the uncomfortable feeling I got in that car was strong that day. Sometimes I could shrug it off. But this time I couldn't, and it snuck up on me out of the blue. It had me turning around in my seat; half wondering if some ball of lightning was going to fall out of the sky. To me, thoughts like that came and went like a thief. It was up to me to discern and sort out the ones that I needed to pay attention to.

I looked up. The sky was warm, inviting and the shade of turquoise. But even than I knew better. Looks can be deceiving, and this bright day was no different. Dad must have sensed it too because shortly after, I remember him turning around and yelling at me to move. As I was doing this, a jagged piece of God knows what had suddenly come crashing into the car. It was a good thing I listened to him.

Had I not, that might have been the end of it right there. But instead, I ended up just having to get stitches on my finger. Though I did get some blood on the car upholstery and I was worried dad was going to get mad at me for that, he never did.

He wasn't mad at all. The rest of the day was a blur, but I always remember the feeling right before the accident. Like a mental tap on the shoulder telling me, *hey-wake up!* Who was it and where was it coming from? That was anyone's guess, but I wanted to find out.

My little dog Buttons agreed with me about the car; he never got in it. Mom always had to play tag and try to catch him if she wanted to take him for a ride. Sometimes I noticed Buttons sitting a few feet from the car and growling. My dad sold it right after the accident. No love lost on that one. I think mom may have been happy too, but she never openly voiced her opinion on it, I could just see it in her eyes.

A GREY RESORT

So here I sit in my grandparents' living room. They have a large picture window overlooking the grounds of their summer resort. There's a beautiful view of the lake, and you can easily see cabins one through four nestled in neat rows at the edge of the lake, several yards apart.

My grandma always kept that window spotless; it always seemed like there was never a window there. But I put my finger on it anyway, just to make sure. I was always testing things I probably shouldn't have.

The birds liked to test the window too; they were always trying to fly in. The loud sound of them hitting the window always made me jump in my seat. I thought about saying something about it to grandma, that sort of thing didn't seem good for her, grandpa, or the birds.

My grandparents looked like they were getting ready to say something important. Grandma's face looked rather terse and not her usual, casual self.

"We've decided that were going on vacation to Florida this year."

Grandma and I were like two birds of a feather; she knew that I probably wouldn't like the idea that she was going away. And she looked worried. I mentally counted how many states there were between Florida and Wisconsin. Too many to count.

I could certainly understand why they would want to go. January winters are horrible in Wisconsin. Brutal, unforgiving, and lasting way longer than any season has a right too. Every spring the whole town would be so excited just to see the slightest hope of spring on the ground. I would try and crack the iceberg squares on the ground with my boot, so that I could see a bit of dirt and maybe a sprig of grass or two.

But until then, it was a long wait. We just had to grin and bear the cold car seats, snow drifts as high as your house, and air so frigid it hurt to breathe. When it comes to Wisconsin winters, Mother Nature could shove it.

"Well, I've never seen Florida honey, and Grandpa and I want to go."

Well, Wisconsin sure sounded like the opposite of Florida. And I'm sure it's quite pleasant in comparison to the winter time. I looked over at Grandpa who was staring at their rust-colored carpeting. He looked like he'd rather be at the dentist.

"When are you leaving?"

Grandma replied, "Tomorrow. And we have so many things planned. I can't wait to bring you a bunch of seashells. They're so pretty. You know that some shells have pretty Mother of Pearl streaks in them. And if you hold a shell up to your ear, you can hear the ocean."

Tomorrow? This was not good news. And enough of the seashell talk. It was like someone took the old Grandma and threw her away somewhere. She never talked like that to me before.

And there it was, that eerie feeling again. It had managed to find a way to creep its way back into my life, again. It had been a few years since the minor traffic accident, but there it was; all fresh and familiar. Like an unwelcome guest to a dinner party.

This time it came on in such an overwhelming rush I wanted to get up out of my hard chair and run out of the room. I needed to run outside and get some fresh air. But I also wanted to ride out their silly conversation; maybe I could convince them to stay.

The whole time they were talking, I could feel those leisurely afternoons with Grandma slipping away. If grandma was going to Florida, I knew she wouldn't be coming back. She would be staying there permanently; like in a morgue permanently. Unsettling as this news was, I felt like I needed to say it out loud.

"Grandma, you're never going to bring me back shells."

I hated saying that.

"Well of course we are, we'll be back in a couple of weeks."

"No, you won't!"

Grandpa gave me a sharp look.

"Well, why the heck not?"

He was scary then, but I still managed to blurt out the reason.

"Because she's gonna die over there!"

Did I just say those words? Yep, sure did. There were a few uncomfortably long seconds before anyone spoke. My heavy words seemed to hang around the room like a wool blanket. I looked over at mom and saw what I thought was a flash of recognition, but only for a moment. Had she felt the same way? Well, if she did, she didn't let on because she recovered quickly and pretended everything was back to normal. And I was back to being the young girl with an unusual imagination.

"No, honey, that's ridiculous. They're going on vacation. No one is going to DIE."

You don't get it, and you're all wrong. And two weeks didn't seem like a little vacation to me.

"Honey, your grandma has never seen the ocean. This will be a fun experience for her."

Oh really? You think being cold and dead is a whole lot of fun? Yeah, I bet it's a hoot!

No one was saying a thing, and I could feel the heat rising in my cheeks.

Get out of your chair people, sing Howdy Doodie, DO SOMETHING! Nope. All they did was just sit and stare at each other, and then at me. I could feel the hot tears coming as Grandma came up to give me a warm embrace. That hurt to hug her; I knew it would be my last.

There was no un-planning their vacation, they were going no matter what. I put my arms around her and wished I could have just frozen time. But she was already in vacation mode, I could see it in her eyes. They were glossy and out of focus, probably thinking about how her toes were going to feel on warm, sandy beaches.

"Don't go."

"I'll be back before you know it, honey. Don't worry about me. And be good to your mom and dad."

I managed a halfhearted wave as she walked out the front door. Everything around me felt fake, contrived, in slow motion. My grandfather was high stepping it to the car, and grandma was not far behind. And all I could see was my grandma walking down those cement steps for the last time. Grandma and her dainty feet, that looked like a ballerina.

Our screen porch door always made an annoying slap as it slapped itself against the metal frame. I never liked that door, and right now wanted to rip it off its hinges.

I wish I could tell you I was wrong in my prediction. I want to say that I was just a little girl with an overzealous imagination. And maybe who knows, perhaps it was?

But maybe I have been given a gift. I don't know really, but what I do know is my grandmother never did make it back from

Florida. And I did never see her again. She was killed by a drunk driver. And that's that.

To this day no one had made any mention of my little premonition. In fact, years later, no one seemed to recall me even mentioning it.

BEGINNINGS

The mosquitos were all over me tonight, in my ears, buzzing around my head, and fighting for prime real estate on my toes. But that part was my fault really, all I had to do was put on sensible shoes. But I'm not that type of girl, all practicality and good sense tend to lie with my sister.

I just wanted to get out there and fish, so I could have some bragging rights around on the resort. But from the looks of it, the only person I would be bragging to would be myself. No one else was around the docks this evening; I guess they were all hiding out in their cabins. That was ok with me; I didn't mind being alone, especially when it was out on the lake.

I casted out, reasonably pleased with how far the bobber went. I reeled in slowly and waited, hoping for any yank or tug. I breathed in the night air and accidentally inhaled a few bugs. I coughed them up and looked around wondering how I managed that one. I swear the bugs around here were declaring war on me.

Despite bitter bug taste in my mouth, it was nice to be out on the dock. We had three of them, and this was my favorite because it always felt dangerous to walk on. It was the narrowest and went furthest out into the lake.

The sun was just starting to set, coloring the sky in pretty Popsicle colors of oranges and reds. A nice contrast against the dark pines across the lake. I turned on my lantern and thought about putting on another worm. I peered into my Folgers can and pulled out a fresh nightcrawler.

As I held it up and watched it twist around in my fingers, I thought maybe now was a good time to stop. I had already been here an hour and hadn't even gotten a bite.

The lake around me felt unnatural and still. Tonight, I couldn't even hear the bullfrogs. Usually they were loud this time of night. And it just so happened that no one else was fishing on the docks either. But I didn't mind; I often liked to fish alone.

Off in the distance, I could hear the familiar echoes of the nearby train. It was both soothing and hauntingly pleasant, nice. The sound could lull me to sleep when nothing else could. But even that couldn't shake off my edgy feeling.

I had just gotten my new contacts last week, and my eyes were a wreck. I didn't like the way I looked in glasses, but my right eye was itching so badly I wanted to rip it out and flick it into the lake.

This reminded me of my classmate, Sam O'Neil. His right eye always twitched whenever he talked to me in the hallways. It made it hard to pay attention to anything he had to say. It was all I could do not to stare at his rogue eyeball and tell it to chill the heck out. I think I made him mad, because during the last week of school if he saw me in the halls, he headed in the other direction. I couldn't blame him, but I did blame his eyeball. Maybe it twitched that way all the time, or perhaps it was just me.

The sun had long set now, and with it came a brisk chill that crept down my spine. I set down my fishing pole and tried to dig out my sweatshirt which had bunched up behind me on the bench. It was crumpled up and inside out, and I couldn't get the thing on fast enough.

As I fumbled with the zipper, I could hear a commotion across the other side of the lake. It wasn't that far, maybe 50 yards or so. Lots of ducks liked to hang out there because it was full of wild rice plants.

A few of my things were scattered about on the dock. I could be a real pig if I wanted to, and today was no different. I cursed at myself for all the messiness, wondering how I made such a mess in such a short amount of time. I picked up what I could with shaky hands, and questioned my urgency to leave.

Those ducks were having a field day over there. I went over in my mind all the different kind of animals that could make that noise. Maybe a deer might have fallen in and was now having problems getting out. Now the sound seemed to be headed in my direction. But really, a deer falling in the lake? Not likely.

I tried squinting to get a better look, but it was already too dark for that. Maybe this was why everything seemed off. As I stood there questioning, I could feel the hairs on the back of my neck stand at attention.

I didn't know what was going on across the lake, but it just felt different. As I got a better look, I could see this was no animal. It looked human, but this didn't ease my mind for long.

Whatever it was, it looked like it was swimming with a Halloween mask. I started backing up on the dock a little too quickly and fell over on my tackle box. Great, why not just fall right into the lake and greet it that way?

It was coming towards the dock, this was clear. I wasn't positive, but I thought it was a he. I could see the eyes, and that's what scared me the most. I wanted to drop everything and make a run for it.

Whoever this was, he made swimming look effortless. Clearly, he wasn't from around here. If he were, he would have been more concerned with crazy John. Every local knew about John and his need for speed when it came to his boat. He always drove it straight down the middle of the lake, not giving a care in the world to anyone else on it. It was pedal to the medal with him, flooring it like a bat out of h-e-double toothpicks. And he always did this at various hours in the evening.

He was so close now I could see his breath in small cloudlets just above the surface of the water. My breath caught in my throat as I finally could see the rest of his face. He was older than me, and his eyes didn't look normal. He was striking, but in a psychopathic kind of way.

Even staring for a moment, I felt almost hypnotized by his face. It felt funny to think this way, but it was true. His hair was dark and slicked back from the lake, casting his skin an unnatural grey. I couldn't tell if that was just him, or from the moonlight. I'm hoping it was the moonlight.

He didn't look like the night air was affecting him at all. I tried my best to meet his gaze, but his stare was too piercing, I looked away. I could still hear him treading water, so I quickly took another glance in his direction. His head was inches above the level of the lake, and sure enough, he was staring right at me. I wanted to tell him to take a picture it lasts longer, but somehow I didn't think he would appreciate that. I did manage to yell out.

"What????"

My word sounded shrill in the night air, and I regretted saying it. I felt the need to explain myself, but again I wasn't the one swimming like a psycho across the lake. Something was unsettling about the mechanical way that he moved.

Well great, here I am, about to be killed off by half robot, half human Olympic swimmer. Maybe he was wondering if I was worth the effort. His eyes were getting brighter the longer he was staring. It was to the point now that it hurt to look into them. I covered my face as best as I could, but I could still feel the heat of his eyes on my arm. How could eyes do that? I could feel the skin on my arms burning, and I couldn't help but shout out.

"Ouch! KNOCK IT OFF!!"

The intense light turned off, and that's when I noticed the pale shade of his eyes. And just a touch darker than his skin. I had never in my life seen eyes that color before. It was so unusual to see up close, all I could do was just stare.

We watched each other for a few moments. And I wondered if he would say something. I wanted him to. As I took a step closer, he backed up in the water. He lingered there a moment longer, then slowly went under. He never once blinked or took his eyes off me. I tried to follow the spot where he went for as long as I could, squinting my eyes against the dark evening.

I watched his light go down into the water, and so faint I eventually couldn't see it at all. He had made no sound whatsoever, no splash, no swirling of water, nothing. I stood there for a moment, straining to see if I could hear him come up elsewhere around the lake.

But I didn't hear a thing. It was if he had never appeared in the first place.

The air around me felt heavy and warm, and the scent of burning electricity ran throughout. I kneeled down and peered over the edge of the dock, touching the water with my fingertips. It was warm as a bath.

This whole thing felt somewhat convoluted to me. The look in his eye felt like he could tear me to shreds. I wondered what his voice sounded like. Now it appears, I would never know.

Sounds of life were starting to wake up around the shore. The frogs came back alive, making kerplunk sounds as they hopped into the water. The waters' temperament had switched gears; from lucid to choppy. More in keeping with its regular self.

With shaky hands, I closed up my tackle box and packed up the rest of my things. I could hear mom calling me up to the house. That was typical mom, her timing was always off. But her yell had broken the spell, and I was glad for it.

"Coming."

I could hear the edges of the lake lapping up against the dock behind me as I made my way up the dirt path to my house. My feet felt like weights, and I couldn't make them move. The corner of my tackle box caught the metal walk pole along the way. I'm sure at this point I've awoken every sleepy person on the resort.

I couldn't shake the feeling of being watched. In that one moment, it felt like he took a small peek into my soul. I was shaky and nervous, but for the first time in what seemed like forever, I felt very alive.

That was the start of my summer in 1984.

FISH-A-WHILE RESORT

*W*ay up in the northern part of Wisconsin, there lies a sleepy little town called Neelsville. Its population is only around 3,000 people, give or take a few hundred or so. And this hasn't changed much.

Neelsville is the kind of town city folks liked to make fun of, but really, it's not much different than any other small town in America. The ratio of bars to anything else averages ten to one. The few stores we do have sell the usual touristy type things; T-shirts, candles, coffee mugs, specialty candies, and maybe a pair of moccasins or two.

A few miles outside of Neelsville, you'll see different billboards announcing its presence. They all look like they were painted a lifetime ago, the colors just different variations of the color Grey. Those billboards are reminders of a long faded, bygone era. My favorite one is the fisherman standing knee deep in water, holding his fishing pole while smoking his pipe. Looking like a cross between Popeye and someone who's pickled himself all afternoon with shots of Whiskey.

If you venture down our main street and make a left just after the post office, you'll see the man who founded Neelsville painted on the side of a building. It looks a bit weathered, the painted face now faded and peeling. He looked to me like Santa Claus, minus the holly jolly.

If you want to buy something other than the usual staples of bread and milk, like dry ice or a particular deli salad, you would have better luck driving 30 minutes south to the nearest Walmart. It's the supercenter and a blessing for the people of Neelsville, though most would not admit it.

We have a McDonalds, a Kentucky Fried Chicken, Dairy Queen, and a Pizza Hut. And that's a big deal for our town. On opening day Pizza Hut had free pizza and drinks for everyone. The crowd of people waiting in line trickled down almost to the bridge at the beginning of the town.

A lot of standing for a free soda and slice of pizza. I was one of the first waitresses that they hired as soon as the building was finished. I was so nervous that first day as a waitress, I didn't stop moving from table to table. The restaurant had smelled so good from fresh pizza being made, and there was a buzz from all the people about this new place.

We have one functioning light on the main drag and a local theatre. One of the best things about Neelsville is my parents' summer resort, which is located 5 miles outside of town. I know I am lucky to live on it because our house is just mere feet from the lake. I have a great view of the water right from my bedroom window. They don't make homes that close to the lake anymore, unless of course you know the right person to get you the proper permits.

My parents bought the resort from my grandparents when I was little. And everything about it and the town has an off the beaten path kind of feel. It's what I like most about it. The people here are a little weathered, but friendly and hard working. I don't know if it's all the pine trees, woods, or just the lake itself. But when you venture this way, it feels like you've stepped back in time.

Most people come to stay at our resort do so to get away from their jobs and do some serious fishing, swimming, or experience what life is like in the North woods. Our resort sits on 5 acres of land, with eight cabins scattered about on the grounds. We have a dirt/gravel driveway that leads to each cabin. Each cabin now looks fresh and new since my parents put a fresh coat of yellow paint on it last summer. Cabin two has the best view of the lake, and also a sweet wooden swing right in front of it; the perfect place to watch the sunset.

Cabin four is tucked away in the middle of a few trees, and the most private. Cabin five is the most popular with families because it has the most extensive layout; and the best view of the pool. It's also my favorite. The resort requires lots of daily upkeep, which keeps my sister and I busy with chores.

We have a pool located right in the middle of the resort grounds. It's a perfect place for it, and where everyone tends to congregate. It's about 9 feet at its deepest point, which isn't bad. But ever since my babysitter nearly drowned in it last summer, it lost some of its luster to me. She had ventured too close to the deep end on a sunny day last July. I wasn't very far from her, only a few feet in fact, because I was lying on top of our cement sun deck.

I remember that day well. It was the first real hot day and a great chance to get a tan, which I desperately needed since I looked about as white as paint. Wisconsin summers never really get too warm, so it felt good to soak in some of the warm rays for once. I happened to look over and noticed something floating in the pool.

At first, it looked like maybe a giant pool float. It didn't occur to me that it could be a live person.

Not knowing how to swim was such a strange notion to me. For as long as I could remember, I always knew how. I guess I took it for granted that everyone else could swim too. My babysitter was such a pleasant person to be around, someone you enjoyed keeping company with because she always made you feel better. She seemed to have more patience than the average person, and she had a smile that warmed up the room. Her hair was dreamy like long, and she always wore it straight with no barrettes or anything like that. Whenever I saw her, she always reminded me of an angel.

When I first realized that it was a person floating in our pool and not some puppet I just froze. Seeing something like that can do strange things to you. You either go into action, or you become paralyzed. On that day, I did the latter. The only reason I knew it was the babysitter was that I recognized her swimsuit, it was a one piece, and it was the color of pea soup.

All I could see was her long hair all splayed out around her like she had stuck her finger in a light socket. It was startling to see, and I couldn't get my brain to work or my feet to move. It was like I was tethered to the ground. Thank God that dad was nearby testing out pool chemicals. He quickly dove in and got her out of the pool. He laid her on the cement with the aid of a couple of others on the resort. He promptly did CPR, and thank goodness, that was enough to bring her back from wherever she had gone.

Every once in a while, I still play out the events in my head, and wonder what could have been had things turned out differently. And not one of those scenarios would have been good for my parents or the resort. So, the pool wasn't high up on my list of things to do. Unless of course, the weather decides to change its mind and turn humid, I wouldn't be using it too much this summer.

I liked walking around the resort best in the morning. There was always smells of fresh bacon and yummy goodness swirling around in the air. The main house I live in sat just feet from the lake, which is called Alice. The water in this lake looks just like coffee and trickles on for miles. It's packed full of wild rice plants, lily pads, and any species of fish you can imagine. You can swim in it, but I wouldn't advise that you do. I have gone swimming in it several times, but I have a knack for finding that straggly piece of seaweed that likes to graze my foot. Not fun to experience when you can't see what it is.

All types of people come here to stay, and from all different walks of life. Some are used to living in the woods, others aren't. You can always tell the ones who aren't the locals. They complain the loudest about the mosquitos, and how our grocery store doesn't have anything to eat.

People also come here to do their fair share of drinking, whether they're a local or not. All the bars are hot spots, but the one closest to us is the Lake Edge Bar. This bar is owned by a lady named Margie Marie. I think her favorite thing in life is tending to her bar. She always has a smile on her face. But I think her second favorite thing is her love of hairspray. Her hair is typically piled on top of her head and sits oddly off to the side, and never a strand out of place. She reminds me of one of the Whos in Whoville. Whenever I walk near her bar, I half expect to see the Grinch hiding out behind a tree.

Saturdays on the resort are always change-over days, which means that the visitors who have stayed the past week finally leave.

There are a few hours in between for cleaning, and then the new visitors come to check in and visit.

So, when we get our new batch of people on Saturdays, my sister and I always like scoping them out. The boys around town didn't pay much attention to me. They only really cared if you had a big chest and were *easy*. I was a no in both areas, so there you have it.

Sometimes I helped clean cabins, but my primary job was to bail out our eight fishing boats. They were always overflowing with water every few days because it frequently rained in our neck of the woods. I remember soaking up every drop of water with my huge mustard colored sponge. I often wished I could just flip it over and be done with it. It rained a lot in Neelsville, so I was always bailing out boats with my sister.

I was also in charge of taking care of the resort's game room. It sat off to the side of our pool. It was the last section of our three-car garage. My dad cleaned it up, put new paint on the walls and added a pool table, pinball machines, and a comfy couch. It was a fun little place. But lucky me, I ended up having to clean it, which included emptying out the ashtrays every Saturday.

Most of our visitors were from the Chicago and the Rockford area. They liked getting away from the hot confines of a city. There was one particular family that liked to visit each year that I was fond of. Especially a particular guy that came with them.

Dad spent a good part of his Saturday mornings sitting on his lawnmower. Mowing the resort usually took a good two hours, and on top of that he also had a regular job, so I never really saw him that much. But we did have a little routine that we perfected. He would be sitting on his mower in blue jean cut-offs and no shirt, yelling for me from across the resort to get him a beer and cigarettes.

I never saw anything else that summer, and I couldn't help but feel disappointed. It would have been nice to see him again. The one in the lake. I had so many questions, how did you hold your breath for so long? Where did he end up swimming too? Now the whole thing just seemed like some weird, over the top dream.

Except it wasn't a dream, it happened. And knowing that I possibly would never see him again filled me with such emptiness that I willed myself to just not even think about it.

The rest of the summer came and went, and before I knew it; the leaves were turning their fall colors. It wouldn't be long before Neelsville would be covered in a blanket of snow.

BUS DRIVERS

Wintertime has a way of overstaying its welcome here in Neelsville. The days tend to drag on in an endless sea of cold and grey. February is the worst; I've always hated it. By then all the snow banks are dingy and yellow. You would have thought every dog in town had christened their own snowbank. To me, it felt like everything and everyone were colored over with a grey crayon.

On days like this, I wondered about the lake and what was in it. My mind wandered, and it wanted to be elsewhere. I didn't want to be in a classroom studying Algebra. I felt like a permanent hiccup had kept me from enjoying my life. I wanted to tell someone what I saw, and I wanted to see him again.

I didn't know how to bring up the subject, and I didn't know what people would say. First of all, nothing unusual ever happens in Neelsville. Our town is a very practical and analytical place. People here are no-nonsense and hardworking, and they especially like their privacy, and minding their own business. Well, for the most part. I won't include the owner of Chick-Dee's Hair Salon.

After a workday, people went home and did what people do. They were polite. There wasn't much value on imaginary ones that swam about in the lake with cartoonish looking eyes. In fact, dreams of any kind didn't seem to fit in here. If you didn't work at the lumber mill or the Harley Davidson plant, you were working at the grocery store or a gas station for minimum wage. Which is ok, you can learn to live with that here.

What you couldn't afford you ended up hunting to get your food. But I didn't want to just scrape on by, and I didn't want to work at the lumber mill. So, my dreams were to leave. At least they were until I saw him. Now what I saw at the lake was all I could think about.

Sometimes I would spend an afternoon on the hill right next to our house and look out at the lake. Willing something, anything to come up out of it. I knew nothing would come of it, but I still tried. I knew he wouldn't dare come out in the daytime where he could easily be seen. A couple of times I thought I might have seen something, but it always ended up being nothing.

Bus rides to and from school were torture for me. I hated riding the bus, and because we lived out in the country, it took a long time to get home. During the winter months, it would get dark quickly here. And the heaters in the bus didn't work very well, it was never warm enough.

By mid-afternoon when it was time to ride it home, it always had that bologna and BO smell.

Our first bus driver was Bruce. He had that carny look that made me take notice. He always wore the same pair of drab olive-green army pants with black military style boots. I doubt he was ever in the military, but he sure seemed obsessed with looking like he was. Bruce also had a quick temper. I didn't think he liked driving the bus much, and my instincts were to stay clear. Bruce looked mighty close to losing a screw.

This was confirmed one snowy day in January when he decided to pull us all over on the side of the road. The kids in the back of the bus thought it would be cool to throw a handful of chewed up licorice down the bus aisle. But instead of hitting one of us, of course, it had to hit Bruce right smack in the back of his neck.

I could almost see hot steam tooting out of his ears as he started grinding the heck out of the bus gears getting it to come to a sudden stop. He jumped out of his seat, while I slumped down in my mine. I wished I were somewhere far away.

I noticed up ahead there was a large snow bank. Instead of pulling over to the side of the road like a reasonable person, he decided to try and leapfrog the bus over it. The result was to get stuck, of course; which is precisely what he wanted to do. So here we are stuck sitting on a lopsided bus. I braced myself for what was yet to come. Making Bruce mad wasn't something I wanted to experience.

I looked out the window and could see a few ice fishermen out on the lake. I wanted so badly to be out there with them, hiding out in a shed; having some peace and quiet. Instead, I was cooped up in a stinky bus, with an unbalanced bus driver.

Just looking at his face made me start to worry about our safety. If all it took was some thrown candy to get him off his keister, he had NO BUSINESS driving a bus full of kids. Especially *our* bus. The kiddos on it were raving lunatics in my opinion. We had a pair of roughnecks who liked sitting in the back and loved to terrify anybody else that dare sit near them. I hated seeing them, and I wished one of their parents would have ended up driving them to school. But, according to the neighbors, no one in that family knew how to drive, and the one family member that did had their license revoked.

Bruce had turned off the bus engine, and for added measure, he decided to let down every window on the bus to make it even more frigid. But this took a few minutes for him to do. I held in a nervous giggle as I watched him go from seat to seat, manually opening all the windows. As he made his way to mine, I scooted my legs as far over as I could. I didn't want any part of him making contact with me.

I noticed sweat stains the size of dinner plates under his armpits, and he reeked like a rotten sneaker. Every few minutes he would start another coughing fit, and I wondered if he was going to have a heart attack. As the cold air began swirling in, I tried not to concentrate on the fact that I had to pee since 4th period. I skipped going to the bathroom because I thought I could hold it. Wrong choice.

I wondered what Bruce would have done if I peed my pants on that stinky bus. I would never give him that satisfaction of course, but how long could you hold it really? It was getting to THAT point.

I wondered how he got this far in life without having a heart attack. For all I knew, maybe he had. I did an excellent job of not laughing out loud or peeing my pants. Considering how dire my bladder situation was, I think I deserve an award.

It took a few worried moms (including mine) to call the office inquiring why their children were not home from bus 59 yet. After what seemed to be a half hour, Bruce started up the bus, and we got home without further incident. However, the damage had been done. He received so many complaints from parents that day that he ended up losing his job. Bruce never drove a school bus again, at least not any in Neelsville.

Our new bus driver was a lady named June. When I first got on, I couldn't see much of her face; it was completely taken over by sunglasses. Her hair was long, with threads of wiry grey running through it, like it didn't know which way to be on her head. She never smiled, but I caught her once laughing at something she was thinking about while driving, and she didn't have much for teeth. The few she had were the color of dark honey. All that was needed to complete the picture was a giant wart on the end of her nose. From the first day I saw June; I couldn't help but think I was looking at a witch.

We had a girl on our bus that looked to be close to three hundred pounds, and she was nine. Her name was Pam, and she was in the fourth grade. Whenever June came to her bus stop, it took Pam longer than usual to get up to a walking position from her seat. And then another couple painfully long seconds to walk down the bus aisle.

I always hated this bus stop because the kids in the back would be hooting and hollering. They caused such a fuss you would have thought they had found a shiny quarter stuck somewhere in the bus seat. They liked throwing things too, and this time they had thrown a pool ball in the air, which landed smack in the back of Pam's head.

A POOL BALL. Those things aren't the least bit light. In fact, if I were Pam, I would have had no problem charging those hooligans for assault. However, it just didn't work out that way. In fact, she didn't even turn around; she just kept on walking down the aisle and off the bus.

Unlike Bruce, June did not stop the bus and wait to figure out who might have thrown the pool ball. To tell you the truth I don't even think June gave a rats a** about it. Blatant disregard at its finest. She just didn't care. Period. She just kept looking out the window and looked like she was mumbling something. For all I knew, she could have been muttering some spell. At this point, I really couldn't blame her.

I glanced over at Peter Richardson who was sitting two seats away. Now Peter was a different breed of a person. He had his own seat because everyone was smart enough to know not to sit there. It was littered with everything from half-eaten salami mayo sandwiches, bugs, or other things you'd rather not think about. I don't even know if anyone bothered to clean it. I didn't think so because the same stuff was seen mucking up the same seats into the next school year. That would explain a lot about our bus and its lingering smell.

Peter was one of those teenagers that had grown into a full-grown adult by the age of twelve. And like clockwork, his finger would start digging in his nose as soon as his bottom found his seat and slid over towards the window. The other unfortunate ones that had to sit near him would sometimes dare each other to stare at him, which was never a good idea.

Peter got a charge out of flicking his undesirables onto the people that were brave enough to stare at him for longer than a few seconds. I only had to witness this once and from then on avoided Peter and the back of the bus like the plague. I just would sit somewhere in the middle and did my best to blend in, be invisible. This is what I wish I could be.

It had now been almost a full year since I had seen the strange guy in the lake. And with every day, hopes of seeing him again were fading away.

MARGIE SUTTON

*M*argie owned the corner bar down the street on Pony Road. It was the usual stop for many of the fishermen at the end of the day, and popular with everyone here. I had been to her bar several times. Dad always asked me to go there to pick him up a bottle of Kessler's and a carton of smokes for the week. He would always call her ahead of time, to make sure it was ok. And the answer would still be the same, "Sure Rich."

She owned two Mastiff dogs, Adam and Eve; they never seemed like dogs to me, they were more like small horses. As soon as I turned the corner from Pony Road, I could always hear them kicking up a fuss from inside the bar, ready to rip the screen off its hinges. She had already gone through a couple of screens. I swear they could smell my fear a mile away.

Adam and Eve were not shy about climbing their way up your shirt like they were climbing a tree. Leaving it stained with muddy paw prints. This happened the second my foot touched the inside of her bar. You would think by by now I would know enough to put on a crappy shirt if I was going to her place. I guess I was just hoping that maybe Margie would have the good sense to come to the door first.

Nope.

I found the rusted handle on the screen door and braced myself for what was coming.

"Hey, Margie."

I didn't want to step further; her dogs were growling and showing their teeth.

"Margie??"

She called them off, and they finally retreated. I think they were looking forward to plowing me down.

"Well hiya, gal. How we doing today?"

"Pretty good."

Margie always had such a pleasant, joyful tone to her voice. It always surprised me because it didn't fit in with the dreariness of her bar. I always hoped that she would spruce it up a little. But she didn't, and maybe that was part of its charm. I guess she was the ornament. She was wearing another one of her bold printed flower dresses and walking with a cane. Lately, she seemed to be relying on it more and more.

"Let me take a good look at ya." She eyed me up and down. "You're sure growing like a weed young lady."

Everyone was always telling me that I was growing like a weed, these same ole people who saw me every few days. At that rate, my head would've been in the clouds by now. Her dogs were still in front of me, and they weren't budging.

"Get out of here you two." She said as she threw them a bone. I breathed a sigh of relief as they bolted out the back door, chasing down the dirt path to the lake.

"Nice day isn't it?"

"Yeah."

"I bet Harvey and the boys are going fishing tonight. It looks like it's going to be a good night for it."

It was always a good night for fishing on Alice Lake. But that's not what I cared about.

In all of these years living on the lake, she's had to have seen something, right?

Margie had lived above her bar most of her adult life. She's been on this lake forever, in all that time she had to have seen something that didn't look right. Folklore, stories, anything. But asking would be the hard part. Margie was as no-nonsense as they came, and despite her age, I still think she would have made a perfect drill sergeant.

I guess with her I would just have to spit it out. But I didn't want her to think I was starting to think a little sideways. Information like that had a way of getting around. I noticed a leftover customer from the night before trying his best to stay seated and upright on his bar stool. His cowboy legs were trying to balance him out, but he was still two seconds from hitting the floor.

His eyes were closed, and he was humming ever so softly an old Willie Nelson tune. I recognized it; my dad was a big fan of Willie Nelson. But he still looked half asleep, despite the fact he was holding a lit cigarette. He stopped his humming and opened his eyes to mumble something I couldn't hear to Margie. He must have ordered one of her pickled eggs because she was unscrewing the lid off her huge canning jar full of them, that sat on the edge of her bar.

Margie's pickled eggs were famous around here, and her over-sized canning jar was always the second thing I noticed while walking into her place. (The first was Adam and Eve). I watched as her hand took a swim into the jar, trying to grab at one of the runaway eggs with her chubby fingers. Why bother with tongs? Her fingers were dredging up all the black peppercorns, swirling them around like they were floating pieces of dirt. I thought maybe this was as good as time as any.

"Margie, have you ever seen anything weird around here?" She looked up from the jar, frustrated at not getting an egg yet.

"Weird? Well, this town is full of that. You'll have to be more specific."

I watched as she grabbed an egg and placed it on a saucer right next to the night of the living dead. Her hand was dripping wet. Seeing all that visually made me take pause on wanting to eat hard-boiled eggs again. As she dried off her hands, Mr. Barstool s-l-o-w-l-y set down his cigarette and tried an unsuccessful attempt at getting a salt shaker. I thought I would save him a few steps and pushed it closer to his plate. It took him a minute to figure out where it might have gone.

"Um, I don't know, anything strange in the water maybe?"

Margie grabbed a nearby rag and wiped up the rest of the pickled juice.

"The lake? Hmm, can't say that I have."

"Oh, really? No Muskie eating a poodle or anything like that?"

That rumor went around for a while. I think it was just a parent's way of getting kids to come out of the lake when they were tired of watching them swim.

Marjorie turned her head towards the window.

"You mean like the Loch Ness monster or something?" She started chuckling.

The man on the stool was showing signs of life. He stabbed a cocktail fork into his egg and took a bite.

"No, nothing like that."

Margie got a little twinkle in her eye.

"Well, I did see a few kids skinny dipping last night. Got quite an eyeful there. They were under the bridge, thinking they were all sneaky."

"Oh."

I wished Margie would have stopped right there, but I was trying to be polite. And I also made a note not to hang around the bridge after dark.

"People forget that I'm the nocturnal sort. And the night has all sorts of secrets to tell."

I believed her.

"Darling, this lake is full of people who fish and swim, that's what it's here for.

"Yeah, I know that, but this was just rather, unusual."

"How so?"

"Well, it looked like some guy but, he had this strange light in his eyes. And then he went underwater, and he was gone. I couldn't see him at all."

I felt funny telling her that. She's going to think Rich's daughter went nuts, but I had to tell somebody. I tried to figure out what she might be thinking, but it's hard to get a good read on poker face Margie. She stood there and looked out the window.

"Well, a person can hold their breath a pretty long time. It just takes practice. And darling, you probably just didn't see him come back up from under the water. He probably swam across the lake to the other side, and you just didn't see him, honey."

I had a hard time believing that.

"Yeah, maybe it was just someone swimming."

Because gorgeous guys with laser-like eyes swim here all the time.

"People love swimming in this lake, but I don't care to. Never seemed right to swim in crazy brown water where ya can't see the bottom!"

Now that was something Margie and I could agree on.

"Say, how was school this year?" She said changing the subject.

"Pretty good. Kinda glad to just be done."

"Well, you've got a good head on your shoulders. Good imagination too, don't ever lose that."

"I won't."

My imagination is what was keeping me alive at this point. I couldn't help but feel disappointed. She was not going to give it another thought. I don't know why I thought this to be surprising. I grabbed the crumpled brown bag full of dad's whiskey and cigarettes and turned to leave.

"Hey, make sure to tell Rich I said hello."

"I will Margie, thanks."

I let myself and my wild imagination out. As nice as Margie was, I was glad to be alone with my thoughts. There didn't seem to be anyone else around that I could confide in. I guess my secret would just have to stay that way.

I took my time walking back. The stars were starting to peek out from the dark blue blanket of sky. The trees along the road took a darker and more mysterious slant. I still had a good quarter mile walk back, so I quickened my step. I never cared for walking alone in the dark, even if it was just Pony Road.

JUNE

I woke up in the morning and walked down the stairs to see my sister over pouring her milk into an enormous bowl of chocolate Krispies. It looked like one of mom's mixing bowls, but she wasn't paying much attention. Mom was buzzing around the kitchen like she just polished off a 2 liter of diet coke. Dad was outside taking care of the resort. It was the middle of June, and every cabin on our resort was booked, and with that came lots to do.

Mom and Dad were planning one of their parties again. Which meant that mom would be busy prepping the food for the rest of the day. I spied a large frosted cake taking up ample space on the kitchen counter.

"Isn't it cool? Mom picked it up from Neelson's." Patti said.

"Course she did." I muttered.

I walked over and saw that the cake was in the shape of a fish and coated entirely in grey icing. The same color as our cement steps.

"Wow, how can they get frosting in that color?" I asked out loud.

I couldn't help but sneak a taste of it. Despite the dirty looking color, the frosting was sugary delicious. Mom shooed my hand away.

"Stop that! The cake is for the party, I don't want you snacking on it."

What I wanted was to finish all my chores and get outside. Guy Jackson and his family had just arrived a couple of hours ago from Chicago. He and his family had been coming up for years, and for as long as I could remember, I've always had a crush on him.

The problem was, he was a good ten years older than me. I hoped my crush wasn't too noticeable…. but it probably was. I couldn't help but get butterflies in my gut whenever I saw him. It got so bad that I would even get that way by just hearing his name, which I know was utterly ridiculous.

So, Patti was going to have to be my little backup in crime.

"Come on, let's see if the Jackson's got in yet."

She rolled her eyes. Unfortunately, Patti knew all about my affections for Guy.

"You mean Guy."

"Oh, shut up." I laughed as I gave her a playful nudge.

"He could care less about you; he has a girlfriend remember?"

She had a point. Guys like Guy were never single for more than ten minutes. Girls buzzed around them like bees to honey. And if one didn't work out, there was always another one ready to take her place.

And I wouldn't even be in the running. Like I said before, guys around here didn't take notice of me. I was too tall, too long-legged, and also different. They liked the shorter girls that could do perfect round-offs at football games. I wasn't very graceful either…

if I attempted a cartwheel, I probably would look like I belonged in the circus.

I had that sinking feeling that Guy wouldn't be coming alone. In all the years I've known him, he NEVER did. But a girl could always dream. Last year he had come up with a girl named Sasha. I think that was her name…or Tara or Farrah or one of those other types of names. She was impossibly gorgeous of course, lovely hair, and a perfect little nose to go with it….just your regular, competitive nightmare. And she wasn't a hundred feet tall like I am.

If I could describe myself, I probably looked a bit like Olive Oil from Popeye, minus the dark hair. I didn't get too particular in what I wore over the summer, but I was usually either barefoot or stubbing a toe in flip-flops every two minutes.

And Sasha, Farrah what's her name was twenty-six and fresh out of law school.

Isn't that wonderful…

Groan...

And here I was, glued in place in my *never-ending* late teens. Bedtime by 9:30.

Yuck.

Patti and I walked up to cabin five. Guy and his family always stayed in that cabin for as long as I could remember, (I always considered it their cabin no matter who stayed in it the rest of the season). It was the biggest and nicest. It had three huge bedrooms with walk-in closets and two good sized bathrooms. And not to mention, a perfect view of the woods across the street. It was also my favorite cabin on the resort.

Whenever his family left and before the cabin was cleaned, I would sneak into it and one of the bedrooms. I knew which one was his from the smell of his cologne. I would smell it on the comforter and pretend he was still there staying at the resort. But all I'd have to do was walk past the closet and see the empty wire hangers, the harsh reality that they were gone.

My heart skipped a beat as I saw his Blue Monte Carlo parked in the dirt drive.

Yay! He was here! And he would only be sleeping a few yards from our house. For a whole week! Oh, thank you, Lord!

Patti must have read my mind. She gave me a little nudge.

"Well, lover boy's here, better break out the lip gloss."

I nudged her back as we ducked into the game room.

"Let's not make it so obvious."

"Well, what do you want to do?"

"I don't know."

"I'm not standing around here waiting for lover boy to make an entrance."

"Well, I'm not either just hold your horses for two darn seconds. You know it doesn't take him long before they'll be at the pool. Will bump into him there."

I'll just conveniently have to check the pool temperature or something like that. As the owner's daughter, I'm just making sure our resort guests are completely satisfied with their swimming experience.

I couldn't wait to see him and wondered about how he might have changed from the year before. I just didn't know *if I* was ready to be seen. I tended to get so flustered around him. But I had been waiting for him to come up since school got out. It would be nice to see him finally. Patti broke my thoughts.

"Why don't you just go up and knock on his door. I know, you could tell him to go get his pole because the fish are biting."

I rolled my eyes.

"Oh, I'll bite you if you don't shut up!"

As we stood in the game room, we heard two voices walking up, one of them sounding nicely familiar.

And I knew that voice anywhere.

But of course, there was another voice along with his.

Groan. And it was female.

Of course, there would be a girl involved. How foolish of me to think otherwise.

I snuck a peek out the game room window, and sure enough there he was, and if I'm not mistaken, a bit taller than I remembered. And there was the girl. Why should I be so surprised by this? But she was different from the one he brought last year. Patti noticed, too.

"Hey, it's a different one this year." she said.

She was different. Wow, I couldn't believe it. I thought Sasha was the one. Huh, I wonder what happened. This girl looked much of the same though. She was wearing some neon colored two-piece. I watched as she turned to give him a big smile. I could tell she was pretty into him, and with that came the sinking feeling in my chest. I could never catch a break.

As we came up to the pool gates, he was already standing there with his back to me. He was wearing his swim trucks like he always did. It didn't matter what he wore; he always made it cool.

His hair looked perfect too. Made me want to run my hands through it.

Wow! Did I just think that? Naughty girl.

He turned around as soon as I came walking up. So much for being sneaky.

"Well, if it isn't stretch."

I hated the nickname, but I was happy that at least I had one.

He took a quick drag of his cigarette and blew it suggestively to the side. This was signature, Guy. I really couldn't stand the smell of cigarettes, but I could overlook it.

"Looks like you grew some since last time."

"Yeah, I guess so."

I looked down, embarrassed. It was hard talking to him, and my cheeks were getting redder by the second. God, I hated that I couldn't control that. I felt like an open book. If there was a hole nearby, I surely would have shoved my head in it.

"When did you get in?"

I knew precisely when he arrived at our resort, an hour and a half ago. But he didn't have to know that.

"A little bit ago. It's nice. Glad to be out of that concrete jungle."

"Was the traffic bad?"

That was such a perfect question. Of course, the traffic would always be bad, it was Chicago. "You know, you guys are pretty lucky you don't have traffic lights."

He said this with a smirk.

"Well, not yet. I'm sure we will have them by next year; you know a girl can only dream."

He chuckled at that, making his eyes all shining and dancing. But just then little Miss Banana colored swimsuit had to come walking up, ruining our obvious chemistry.

Groan. I guess it was best to get the pleasantries over with.

"Hey Brooke, I want you to meet someone. This is Lisa."

"Oh, so this is *Brooke* from the resort."

I didn't quite know what to think about her emphasis on my name.

"Yeah, Hi Lisa."

So, what had he told her about me?

She gave me a smug once over and walked over to the edge of the pool, dipping in her toes.

"Ooh, pretty icy."

Well, I could certainly see why they were together, beautiful people always were.

She had a lot of hair, all long and coppery.

I watched as she did a perfect little swan dive into the pool. It was straight as an arrow, barely making any waves. Perfect. I was lucky if I could manage a cannonball.

I was glad when he turned his attention back to me.

"So, how was school this year?"

I looked down. School? What could I say? It was pretty much the same. My main goal was just to get through it. I always seemed to forget where my brain was whenever he spoke to me. So, I mentally said the answer in my head before I said it out loud.

"Oh, it was pretty much the same ole thing, just another year. How was your school year?"

He chuckled.

"I don't go to school silly."

Darn it.

"I mean, you know, work and stuff."

"It's good. You know, it's work."

He gave me another smile. Man, I hated it when he did that. I wondered what it would be like to work with him. I wonder what it would be like to be his secretary. I knew he worked for some financial company, and that's all I knew about it.

"Do you still like to write?"

He remembered!!

"Yeah, just poems and stuff, but yeah I still do."

"Well, that's good. Don't stop doing that, keep working on it, I think that's pretty cool."

"Really, oh well ok. I'll keep writing."

He thought my poems and writings were cool. Maybe there was hope for us yet.

I couldn't help but stare at the muscles bulging up in his arms. They always did when he brought a cigarette to his lips. Maybe the cigarette company should consider him being one of their models. They would probably sell more, that's for sure. I could feel a wave of jealousy come over me, which I did my best to hide. I needed to get my emotions back in check.

"Well, I better get in the water before I get into trouble."

He gave me a little wink and threw out his cigarette. I watched it as it quickly burned out on the hot pavement. I half wanted to pick it up but thought the better of it.

"Yeah, I guess so. Miss Yellow swimsuit is beckoning."

I might have mumbled the last part.

I watched as he swam up to her and grabbed her leg. Her screech echoed through the air, scaring some of the birds.

Time to make my exit.

I turned around and did a massive roll of the eye. I didn't want to be there anymore.

CASSIE DuPREE

We had a very colorful neighbor named Cassie. My mom liked to call her *a real pistle.* She was married to a down to earth man named Lyle. She often called him Lyles, and the name stuck because it seemed to suit him. Their cabin sat close to our resort and looked so luxurious and homey that at any moment you might expect Hansel and Gretel to come walking out looking for candy.

Cassie wasn't from Wisconsin. She was formerly from Florida, and so she was always cold. I rarely saw her without a cardigan draped over her shoulders, and she owned one in just about every color. Cassie's hands always seemed occupied, one with a cigarette, the other with any manner of drink. But I knew her preference was vodka tonic, because I could always smell it on her breath. Not that I was into drinking, but my parents liked to entertain, and I paid attention.

Their cabin sat a few feet up from the lake, and the grounds surrounding it had the thickest blanket of moss all around it. I always liked walking on it barefoot; it made me feel like I was walking on a cloud somewhere. It was in the most eye-popping shade of green that it didn't look real.

Lyle loved to fish. Sometimes I would be busy playing in the backyard, and I almost had a near collision with him. One late evening he was on his hands and knees crawling around on the ground. I thought it odd to see a grown man crawling around like that, like he lost a toy. But I learned something new about Lyle that night. He liked getting on all fours to search out for night crawlers to fish with.

That evening I peered out towards the lake. The lake that was always dark and full of secrets.

I wondered if I would ever see him again. I wondered if he was still out there somewhere.

Still looking, I walked forward but didn't see Lyle who was on all fours just a few feet right in front of me.

Dear Old Lyles.

I did a complete summersault over him. It was either that or fall on top of him, with me probably breaking his poor old back. Well, I didn't want that. I bet if we had it on videotape it would have been hilarious. He was apparently startled but took it with a grain of salt. I was thankful then that Lyle didn't get mad quickly. He probably would have been the perfect candidate to drive our bus.

"It's ok girl."

He brushed his hands together and slowly made his way back up to a standing position. He reminded me of a rugged, good-looking cowboy. He had on a plaid, long-sleeved shirt with mother-of-pearl snaps. The sleeves were rolled up and pushed up to his elbows. He had a faint tattoo that looked like it was drawn with a sharpie; the outline was grey and smudged and the letters were hard to read. I wanted to ask him about it, but I didn't. He looked like he owned these woods.

"What you doing out here in the dark?" He asked.

"Oh, not much really."

"Lookin for something?"

"Um, no not really." I lied.

Seen any strange guys with wild eyes down by the lake?

"Just walking around, hanging out."

"Well, this is the best time to get crawlers. They like coming up this time at night. They like crawling around in the moss. Oh, look at that little devil right there."

He quickly grabbed hold of a worm and gently tugged it out of the ground, being careful not to pull it in half. He did this with the careful precision of a Blue Jay. His old Folgers can looked full of them. I could see them trying to wiggle their way out, like dark, moving shoelaces. From the looks of it, he would have more than enough to fish for tomorrow.

☽

I often liked to pop in to Cassie's place in the summer. I enjoyed hearing her stories about the south, it was interesting to me since I lived in the North all my life.

She had such an infectious laugh and personality. It made one happy just being in the same room as her, and it was hard not to get sucked into it. I never saw Cassie without make-up. She would probably think it sacrilegious. And she was always particular about her shade of lipstick. It was the same bright red color, 'Cherries in the Snow' she called it. She liked telling me this every time she saw me. I was starting to think that maybe she thought my lips were completely devoid of color. When Patti and I walked over there together, Cassie was busy giving her dog, Tootles a bubble bath. Cassie was still wearing her white terrycloth turban for her hair, and still in her bathrobe. But with Cassie, it wasn't that strange to see her still walking around in her bathrobe and slippers in the middle of the afternoon.

Maybe she saw something at the lake too. She seemed prone to supernatural things it seemed. I watched as she shared her vodka tonic with Tootles. That dog will do anything to keep her happy. If anything had ever happened to him, Cassie would probably need electric shock therapy. I looked down at her kitchen tiles and saw part of Tootle's poor tail.

She had given him a fresh haircut and bath, drying him off while doing her puppy baby talk voice. Tootles was having none of it; he turned his face away in disgust. Probably didn't help matters that she drank Vodka like there was no tomorrow and smoked about the same way. Her breath probably as fresh as week-old fish.

"So, what you up to doll?" Cassie was rubbing him senseless with his own Monogrammed "T" towel.

"Oh, pretty good."

I looked over at Patti.

"Remember when you said you'd like to give Patti a make-over?"

Patti was in that very awkward in-between stage where a few makeup tips wouldn't be all that bad. But one thing I didn't envy was her hair. God bless her, but her hair reminded me of a fried tumble-weed. It was impossible to comb without ending up in a foaming at the mouth argument. It was a constant battle dealing with her hair every morning before school.

"Why sure doll. I love make-overs."

She brought out her large tackle-box full of make-up. As soon as Cassie was done with Tootles, she got right to work on Patti.

"Hmm, let me see here. Well, your face could use some color doll. Say, don't you ever let your skin see the sun?"

Patti just sat there looking sheepish. And pale.

"Yeah, I go outside."

"The sun won't hurt ya none. Your skin is damn near the same shade of school glue, ya know, Elmer's."

Cassie's blunt way of talking had a way of blowing things out of proportion. But that was just her way, she didn't mean anything by it. I had to cover a laugh because Cassie was blowing smoke in her face, and I could tell Patti was trying to hold her breath.

"A little color isn't gonna hurt ya."

Patti looked at me like she wanted to slap me silly. I just couldn't wait until Cassie finished her masterpiece.

I watched as she put a layer of foundation all over Patti's face with her little white sponges. I wonder what mom was going to think of this. She probably wasn't going to dig it much.

"Now for some blusha. Give those cheeks a little tweak of color."

Cassie was laying the foundation on a little thick. And the hue didn't seem to match.

"I don't know Cassie; you think that will go?"

"Oh, sure it will doll."

I watched as Cassie finished up. Patti sat there being a good sport.

I thought about maybe asking Cassie if she had ever seen anything weird at the lake. But I just didn't. But I was determined to figure out what I saw. I wasn't going to have another summer go by and not see anything. I couldn't.

I decided that maybe I should look more out in the woods. Look, for him. For some reason, I couldn't help but think that that weird part of the woods and what I saw was related somehow. I just didn't know how.

FISHING HOLES & HANKY PANKY

*M*y dad knew all the secret fishing holes in the area, and where to go to get certain kinds of fish. The crappie liked to hang around in the weeds under the lily pads. Sunfish liked to graze just above the surface of the lake. Bluegills were plentiful too. But deep down in the lake is where the Musky and Northern Pike liked to be, and what people liked to catch most around here. They could get rather large, and after a trip to the taxidermy, they hung like trophies on a wall.

The lake trailed on for miles and miles, and it eventually turned into rapids. We had three docks, and the dock that I liked to fish on was the middle one. It was always the first one to go underwater when the first real rain storm of the season hit. And was also the most in need of repair, but its length went farthest out into the lake. After a rainstorm, the planks of it slipped a few inches below the surface, making it difficult to walk on without slipping. My sister and I would dare each other to jump on it to see how far below the surface it would go. Or who could stand there the longest without slipping into the water. I couldn't believe how much abuse this piece of wood took without ever breaking apart, but it never did.

My parents loved getting people together for any reason. If you wanted to find out who was doing what, who was bringing what item to the picnic, you went to the pool to find out. My mom was very organized when it came to arranging these parties. She walked to each cabin to see what the occupants would be bringing and to remind them again what time the party was.

Of course, they had the option of bowing out, but usually, the lure of my father's guitar and the loud Kenny Rogers music over the loudspeaker would coax anybody out of the security blanket of their cabin. If nothing else, to figure out what the heck all these people were about.

My parents were always welcoming to strangers. In fact, at the end of the night, even the person with the coldest heart and most skeptical eye could be charmed by my dad. And by the end of it, that same person would usually be singing along with him, trying to hum a tune (even though they were probably two sheets to the wind). It was a good feeling, and people ended up more warm and fuzzy then when they arrived, and most of the time wanted to come back again to stay for the next summer. And they often did.

We had eight cabins. Six of them had indoor plumbing; two did not. With those two cabins, you had to walk to the outhouse to do your business. Those cabins were usually occupied by deer hunters. Cabin five was the biggest and had the best view of the pool.

Cabin seven was the most interesting. It was the most expansive, with one of those bedrooms that if you walked through the closet, you could walk straight into the next bedroom. It was creepy though. Right next to it was a large thatch of Rose bushes. Roses are picky to grow, but they never had a problem growing there. There was a shadowy looking tree that stood right next to it, it always seemed like it was guarding the cabin. Its branches sprayed out on top of it as if to say, "It's mine." Ironically, this tree got hit so many times by lightning that mom lost count. The last time it was hit one of the tenants was sleeping on the couch in the front room with the arm of a sweatshirt hanging over the edge of the sofa.

The lightning ended up striking the tree and had snaked its way down the tree trunk, along the window and inside the cabin on the couch. It burned a dark, inky path along the front of a sweatshirt that happened to be in its path, ruining it. It never harmed the person sleeping there on the couch. But it had alarmed them. I remember following the trail it had made with my finger. It looked like a thick, curvy line on a roadmap.

I always thought it funny that mom wrote out a check to the guest that stayed there that week. She ended up reimbursing them for the sweatshirt. She wrote the check out and in the memo stated: *Act of God.*

"Guy, do you believe in the supernatural?"

He was standing there in front of me squinting his eyes. The sun was unbelievably bright

"What do you mean?"

"I mean, like things you can't explain, or things you can't see."

"Well, there are lots of things in the world that really can't be explained."

I watched as he pulled out a cigarette from the pack and lit it with his other hand. He took a small drag and teasingly blew it in my direction. I didn't care much for cigarette smoke but coming from him, I could tolerate it just fine.

"That's rude."

He just smirked.

"I thought I saw something."

He gave me an awkward glance.

"Really? What?"

"I don't know." I wasn't sure how to tell him.

"Care to elaborate?"

"You'll probably think I'm crazy."

He had such a gentle look on his face, it made me want to reach out and kiss him.

"Listen, I don't think that. What did you see?"

"Well, I saw something strange in the water, some guy was swimming. And I don't know; he looked kind of weird. There was this strange light coming from his eyes."

"Well, you probably just didn't see him come up for air. Maybe he was holding a waterproof flashlight."

"Stop."

"Ok, I'm just playin. So, it was a he?"

"I said that."

"Look, Brooke; he was probably kidding with you and he was carrying a light on him, that's all."

"I know, but it was just strange how he went under, and then, just disappeared."

"Sometimes people can hold their breath a long time."

Yes, but he never came back up.

The one thing I did know was there were two things that actually made me feel alive.

One was seeing Guy.

And the other was what I saw at the lake.

A GREY RESORT

There seemed to be a little bit of hanky-panky going on in Cabin 4. Now my mom can sniff out sideways types before their sneaker can hit our pavement. And it first looked like the couple of guys that checked in did so with the intentions of making a fishing getaway. The fishing was always good on Lake Alice. You just really needed to be aware of the stumps, because they were everywhere. My dad used to say that you could connect the dots with a stump every 2 feet on the lake.

But cabin 4 had a strange woman walking real quick like from her cabin with heels on that looked like tiny stilts. Her shorts were uncomfortably too high, and her half top barely covered what it needed to. But it was a warm evening after all, and none of that was my business. But from the looks of it, the fishermen picked up a few night ladies in town.

It became our business when I accompanied my mom the next day. It was change-over Saturday. She needed some cleaning supplies. Pat, our usual cleaning lady, would be a half hour late that day. So, I helped mom bring some of the cleaning supplies to the door.

As mom opened the screen door, the putrid smell of vomit hit our noses like a punch in the face. It was everywhere, dripping down the countertops, in small puddles on the floor, and scattered about the entire cabin. We both stood there in the doorway trying to take it all in. There were just no words. We were both stunned. Someone had a vomit party, and we were not invited.

I covered my mouth and looked around in amazement. We both just stood there in the doorway. I wasn't setting foot anywhere inside of that cabin, and I sure hope mom wasn't expecting me to clean it with her. But I'm sure mom suspected this.

I watched as she unscrewed her big bottle of Pine-Sol and poured a generous amount into the bucket. She was gonna need several of those bottles if it were up to me. She had with her a fresh pair of yellow rubber gloves and started putting them on.

"Why don't you go try and clean the game room a little."

"You sure mom?"

I was beyond relieved.

"Yep. Pat will be here soon."

"I can't believe they left the cabin this way."

That was all mom could say, over and over again. I felt sorry for her then, having to put up with that vile mess. But if I didn't get out of there, I was gonna be sick myself. Right then I decided that I would never own any resort, or manage any type of of hotel. I never wanted to clean up another person's mess. Ever.

BEHIND THE CURTAIN

*I*t was the dog days of summer, and the top of the lake was heavily sprinkled with a spirodela algae bloom. The lily pads and cattails were practically buried in it.

A small collection of clouds had been brewing all afternoon, but other than that, nothing else was moving at all, making the air uncomfortably stagnate. The thick air was inviting every living fly and bug in the neighborhood.

I was walking home from a friend's house, taking my usual path to the West. It was the best one to take if you wanted to avoid the tree farm. And lately, that's exactly what I wanted to do.

A few yards ahead I could hear a few voices in the distance. As I got closer, I quick crouched down behind the nearest tree. There were two men, and I recognized them. They were staying at our resort, both in cabin three. They looked to be around Guy's age, somewhere in their twenties. I could tell by the way they were talking, that they had been drinking. One of them had an ax in hand, while the other one was just standing there smoking.

Why would you bring an ax on vacation?

The one holding the ax was cutting down everything in his path like he was cutting down bush in the jungle, and laughing hysterically while doing it.

Why was he doing that to our property?

I peered around the tree, still down and holding my breath trying to listen to what they were saying. This wasn't going to sit well with my parents; this was our private woodsy sanctuary, not theirs.

Why would he be cutting everything down? I hoped I could tiptoe out of there carefully without being seen. I slipped behind the tree and tried my best to hide. I got as low to the ground as I could without laying on it. I could feel an odd vibration underneath my hands then. I looked around and noticed that the whole ground was shaking. I looked up, and the trees were swaying back and forth.

We don't have earthquakes here in Wisconsin.

The two men had felt it too. I could see them looking at each at each other and around the woods nervously.

My first thought was, good! That's what you get for cutting down our trees! But I was scared too.

They were short of breath, and their panicked voices echoed in the trees.

"What holy hell is that?"

"Don't know."

I held onto the tree that was in front of me. I never felt this before, the ground felt so unstable. It was unsettling, and I wondered if earthquakes were possible this far up North.

I looked over at another vast leafy oak tree that sat right in the middle of the forest. It was the largest one there. It seemed like all this movement and vibration seemed to be coming from it.

I watched it closely. I noticed its bark ever so slowly was turning...different colors??

I swore it was. Now it looked to be grey? How could that be?????

My eyes were playing tricks on me.

From out of nowhere, I could have sworn one of its branches had just moved. Not from the wind or a passing squirrel. But like a snake, slowly slithering its way along the trunk, making its way down to the ground. It was moving like it was ALIVE.

And it was looking for something…

I stood as still as I could. I was so scared; I didn't dare breath.

Trees didn't move like that.

I looked again to see if there was an animal up there.

The only thing that looked like that would be a snake. And this was no snake.

I sat quietly and watched as the tree moved on its own.

This time there was no mistaking it. Every branch was moving like the head of Medusa.

I couldn't believe what I was witnessing. And I didn't move an inch.

This felt like the same fear I had experienced that night on the lake.

I hoped I was far enough away not to be noticed. I didn't want to be anywhere near its path of climbing limbs. They looked hungry, looking to wrap itself around anything that had a pulse.

As the two men stood before it, they looked as if they were getting read their rights. Their backs were to me, and that's all I could see before a powerful burst of light started coming from the tree.

The light looked strange, but also familiar.

I dare not move. I couldn't believe what I was seeing. This looked like something out of a fairytale. The glare from the tree was unbearable. I saw one long-limbed branch gingerly grab the axe out of the man's hand and threw it towards the open sky.

The axe whizzed on past me with hyper-like speed, making a strange whistling noise as it shot on past.

I heard a wolfish growl coming from the direction of the tree. "Stop."

The tree started turning back to various shades of black, brown, even a dark purple in there somewhere, and finally back to its original color of grey. And the branch went back to its normal pre-live state, back to just a tree.

I stared at the branches for the longest time. For now, they didn't move. The two men snapped out of whatever spell they were both under, and started to run. They both went in opposite directions. It wouldn't take them long until they got back to the resort. I didn't know who was more scared, me or them.

The tree came to life.

I started shaking while staring at that tree. It was back to standing still and being all normal and tree-like. Back to what regular trees did, which was just stand there, all massive and majestic, with an occasional sway in the breeze. From that day on, that tree would never be normal to me again.

I was going to die if one of those limbs came back to life again. But I recognized that light.

"You haven't run away?"

I sharply turned to the direction of the voice. I couldn't see anything in front of me, but off to my side, I could hear soft steps against leaves. Whoever it was, it was coming closer.

I held my breath. Should I turn around? I couldn't bear it.

I could only breathe the words.

"Don't hurt me."

"I'm not here to hurt you. Not ever."

I wasn't alone.

I wanted to run away so badly.

"But then you would never know, would you."

"Never know what?"

Curiosity won over; I slowly turned around. There was a strange man in front of me, a young man. And he was standing too close for my liking. I kept thinking how he could have managed that, because I hadn't seen him coming.

He had the gaze of a hunter, and I knew that look. I suddenly felt a familiar sensation in my chest. That strange feeling of warmth and out of my mind horror at the same time. Like a soothing balm mixed in with a bit of dynamite. I wasn't even sure of my feelings now, scared for sure but…

"I would never hurt you."

"Ok, but what do you want?"

Heart palpitating in the chest. So loud that he could probably hear it.

"That's unnecessary to be scared. I was hoping you would come here."

We were right in the thickest part of the woods. Of course, we were. It would still be a good twenty-minute jog to get back to the resort. I eyed his well-built frame and the muscular tone to his arms. Well, he wasn't a stranger to working out. He could probably snap me in half from the looks of it.

I stood for a second trying to figure out what I was going to do.

"I would never do that to you, but you know that already, don't you?"

I decided that I should make a run for it. He was creeping me out acting like he knew what I was thinking. And he had a very *unearthly* quality about him. Like I was standing next to Big Foot or something.

Trees coming to life. Strangers appearing out of nowhere. My life today was a page out of Brothers Grimm.

I was running alright, and every tree branch managed to connect with my face. Legs were getting scratched up with raspberry bushes too. Not that I was feeling anything. I just wanted to get as far enough away as was possible. But at the same time, I felt like my chest was about to collapse.

I was too young to have a heart attack, wasn't I?

All I could see was those crazy, winding tree limbs looking around for something to wrap itself with...

I stepped on something jagged on the ground which caused me to stumble hard on my right side. I fell like a ton of bricks, gasping for breath. Great. Probably stepped on a random piece of glass. What it was doing out in the woods, I hadn't a clue. But there it lay, and of course, my foot had to find it.

I could feel my foot throbbing as I lingered for a moment on the ground trying to catch my breath, and wondering if I should get up. I looked around, but I didn't see anything, not yet anyway. He had to be nearby.

Maybe I could just play dead. Mentally check out.

"You've got quite an imagination."

Why did he keep answering my silent questions? How could he possibly even know what I was thinking?

It was him again, I sensed his presence before I saw him. And there he was. I could see his athletic frame amongst the trees. How did he get to me so quickly? Well, from the looks of him I could tell right away why. He scared me.

I looked down and noticed a fresh gash swelling up on my thigh. I put my hand on it and could feel my pulse. The blood had left my hand all sticky. Slowly, I made my way back up. When I looked up, I noticed no one was around. Why would he be chasing me just to disappear?

The two men that got the fright of their lives were long gone, beating feet back towards the resort, and probably wondering if they needed to check themselves into the nut house. I got up and started walking as fast as I could in that direction.

It was him, the guy at the lake. And if I still wanted to talk to him, now was the time to do it.

But I was scared, and I didn't feel comfortable being alone with him in these woods. Even though, he probably would have hurt me already if he was planning on it…

I had waited so long for this, to see him again; FINALLY. But this was too dangerous, and he frightened me. I didn't like him being this close.

I could sense his movement behind me.

Oh, crap.

To my surprise, someone was standing in front of me. But it wasn't him. It was something else, entirely. Another man, I think, but he looked nothing like the man I just saw. He was….

Darker.

The first thing that was obvious was the way he carried himself, and it was with extreme confidence. The only thing vulnerable looking with him was the way he was drinking. He was holding something covered in a brown paper bag. He looked like a walking wino stereotype. But instead of worn out dirty, clothes, he was dressed in clothes that looked foreign and out of place.

"Funny running into you here."

He talked like I had just bumped into him at the post office.

It wasn't a stretch to say he looked like he fell out of another dimension. He was the sort that demanded attention. I couldn't help but stare.

"You look about as parched as one of your deserts. Would you like a drink?"

This wasn't good.

"No thanks."

My mouth needed liquid in the worst way, but I wouldn't be swapping spit with him.

He laughed.

"Well, considering where I've been, probably a good assumption."

My nerves picked up.

"Did you just hear what I thought?"

"And with infinite ease, I tell you."

He shrugged his shoulders.

"It's just one of my talents, which I have many. What gifts do you have?"

Now there was a question. I felt sick just being in his presence. I half thought I would turn to stone. Everything about him looked dipped in evil. And he looked like he wanted to rip me apart, but his curiosity was stopping him.

I carefully tried to step back.

"No gifts, sorry."

"Oh, but you do know how to tell a rather tallish tale."

He smiled, revealing a brownish mess of teeth.

"You know very well the gifts that you have. Your problem is that you don't know how to use them properly."

Nothing good was going to come out of this. And since I saw him, the only thing I wanted to do was get away. I knew he could sense this. And that wasn't good odds for me.

I thought briefly about how I could sometimes know about people and their futures. Sometimes it was someone close to me, other times it was just strangers in passing. Could that be what he was talking about?

"Bingo."

His eyes were blazing.

"How did you know about that?"

"As I said, I have my talents. But mind-reading is my absolute favorite. Unfortunately, it doesn't work with my kind. Quite fun knowing I still can do it. And even better that it took hardly any effort."

He was sitting on top of a large rock as if he owned it. Eyeing me like prey, while picking at his long fingernails. They were discolored and curled up at the end, like he had been growing them for a LONG time. The thought made me shudder.

Ok, think. How was I going to get out of this?

"But all you humans are so predictable, so easy to figure out. But not you, you're quite a different breed entirely, aren't you? I'd love to see what you can do up close. So how is it done? You see someone, and then you mentally picture their funeral?"

"No. And it doesn't work that way."

"Oh, you're not as lily white as you think you are."

"I never said I was."

I was shaking and wished I didn't say that. The last thing I wanted to do was provoke him. He was already angry.

"You wear your gift like a number on a football player."

"What do you know about it?"

"That it's a silly sport to pass the time."

Ok. Just stalling now. Trying to figure out a plan to get away.

"You can't dear. Better just go with it."

"Go with what?"

"Didn't anybody tell you not to walk alone? Especially out in *these* woods?"

"I live here. Who are you?"

"Well then, this is the first I've come across the likes of you. But then again, I don't venture here often. Time here has a rather dull charm to it, don't you think? Sort of not my speed. I mean, what do you people do all day?"

I tried my best to put on a brave face, but my insides were shaking.

"You're all banged up. Fragile you are. What got you running off into a little tizzy anyway? Did you see the grey?"

The grey? What was he saying? Could he mean that false part of the woods?

"Bingo again, two for two. And don't play all doey-eyed with me. I will always be many steps ahead."

I quick thought about the part of the woods that didn't seem like it belonged. There were small patches of grey popping up here and there out in the field. I dismissed it as something chemical that might have been spilled. What else could it be?

"What are you going to do now? First, you see the live tree, and now I grace you with MY presence. I would say you've gotten yourself in quite a pickle."

"This is my home, and I wasn't bothering anyone. And you never said where you are from."

I was just stalling now. Anything to delay what he was planning to do. Because it probably wasn't anything good.

"Oh, now there's a question. You could say, I'm from the future and the past."

He laughed crazily at that. Like it was the funniest thing he heard all day. He gained back his composure and pointed a long, crooked finger in my direction.

I couldn't help but look down.

"Could you come over here, please. Just for one little moment. I would love to get a closer look at you. It's rare these days that I would even *want* to come in contact with humans. Their usually rather lackluster and uninspiring."

I felt like a youngster getting lured into a strangers car.

I could feel the evil in him, he was wearing it like a coat.

"Perceptive little thing, aren't we? But I wouldn't count it out, being evil can be so much fun."

I hated that he could read my mind. I felt helpless as I took a few steps backward. A snarl came across his face, making him look even more ominous, if that was possible.

"Oh, come on, I'm not all that bad. Once you get past the eyes, at least. But it has been awhile since I've properly groomed."

He laughed again, and I couldn't help but run. I ran like I was sprinting the 100-meter dash. I didn't get far. Before I could get even a few feet away, I felt a cold hand grab at one of my ankles;

causing us both to fall hard to the ground. I rolled over trying to get back up, but his hands pinned me down. He laid on top of me, his face inches from mine.

So not a good place to be.

His hot breath smelled like rotten garbage and I was so repulsed, I just closed my eyes. It was all I could do. I wished I could just faint.

"Get off!!" I screamed.

"No one's around darling. Not when I'm here. They don't dare. That's the thing about Mother Nature, it truly knows who's in charge. And it surely isn't you. All you humans collect up like a pile of cheap rubbish. Too many of you if you ask me."

"I didn't ask."

He stopped moving then, and I prayed I didn't tick him off too much. I couldn't help it; my mouth was always getting me into trouble.

"Don't play around with me young lady. Do you know who you're dealing with? Don't you utter one more sound. Do you hear me? You do, and it will be you're very last one here on earth."

I didn't doubt him, I just shook my head. Now would have been a good time just to go ahead and faint already. I didn't know how long I could take him being this close before I would pass out.

I tried to think of things that made me happy then, my grandmothers smile. The way my dad liked to play his guitar and entertain. The way mom always folded our laundry in neat little piles, waiting for me to take up to my room. Simple things, pleasant things. I would always get so annoyed with mom when she had all those piles of laundry. But deep down, I always appreciated it.

"I'm glad we have this understanding."

I turned my head to get away from the stench. He sniffed at my neck.

"You smell like a rather delightful day here on earth."

He licked the side of my cheek. His tongue felt slimy and cold, and that's when I felt very far away. I vaguely felt his saliva run down the side of my face. Some of his strands of hair even fell against my cheek, and they too moved like it was alive. Like the limbs of that crazy tree. Odd. I prayed it would be over soon.

"What do you want?" I said in between clenched teeth.

"I think it's pretty obvious."

I wanted to die. I couldn't believe how quickly his hands moved. They were all over me in rapid like movements, like he was trying to consume as much as he could in as little time. Almost like I was being attacked by a giant reptile.

As if he had never felt a body before.

I lay there paralyzed while he quickly tried ripping off my shirt with his long, yellowed nails. The edges of them dug into my skin and felt as sharp as knives. He started tearing at my shirt but didn't get very far. He stopped suddenly and looked around.

I could hear a massive swoosh overhead but still didn't want to open my eyes.

His attention had turned towards the sky. He was looking up.

"Oh, Christ," he said through snarly teeth.

Whatever it was, it was flying high above us. I heard it land a few feet away. And I could hear his voice before I saw him.

"Get off her."

He didn't budge.

"Right now."

It was the same voice I had heard earlier.

"No. Find your own."

"You heard me."

"Oh, why does your kind CONSTANTLY HAVE TO RUIN MY FUN."

He was suddenly off me within seconds. I looked around, and didn't see him anywhere. Did he fly away? Funny, I didn't recall him having wings. But the other one was still close by...

"I wouldn't have hurt her you know."

He came out of the clearing. And I was immediately relieved to see that it was the same guy I had seen in the lake with the kind eyes. Strange, but kind.

"I said, leave here! Go back to where you came from. There's nothing for you here."

"Oh, but I think there is. Can't you feel it all around us? The beautiful hope of humans? Quite silly really, considering what they have coming to them in the future."

In two swift movements, he was at the thing, and grabbed him by the sleeve and lifted him farther away from me like he was a piece of lint.

I watched as his dark presence flew about in the air, changing form. Looking like a crumpled-up garbage bag, and then finally, back to his dark self.

He recovered quickly, landing on his feet.

"You really don't want to fight me on this, do you?"

The beautiful stranger turned to me.

"You should go."

I tried to hold together my shirt, but all the buttons were hanging loosely by threads. The shirt was a goner.

He turned his attention back to Mr. Black with the dead, red eyes.

"Go now, before I rip you in half. Never come to this dwelling again."

"Do you think you really could?"

Mr. Red Eyes was challenging him. But even so, he seemed a bit off his game and was backing up as he spoke.

The stranger looked like he could do some severe damage.

"Oh, I wasn't planning on staying. This place bores me to high heaven anyway."

With that, he quickly jumped up into the air, straight up. I tried following with my eyes until his form looked nothing more than a black dot in the sky. And then there was nothing.

He was gone.

The sky was back to being blue and scattered with clouds. All around us, there was a foulness in the air. The stranger turned his attention back to me.

"Are you hurt?"

I shook my head no. I wasn't hurt, not really. Shook up, yeah.

Ordinary beings don't fly like that in the air.

Humans don't have red eyes either.

I wasn't ready to make use of my legs yet, or anything else for that matter. I tried getting up, but they were shaky and bleeding. I sat back down on the grass while trying to be modest with my shirt.

He kneeled in front of me, and I could tell he was watching his moves carefully, wondering what he should do next. I just hoped it was nothing terrible.

He was indeed the person I saw at the lake.

Well, it was about time. Better late than never.

But it didn't mean I wasn't scared of him.

"I've seen you before." I trembled while saying this. He edged a bit closer. Usually this would have frightened me more, but considering how he shooed away the other guy; I thought maybe I was in good company.

But I was still alone with him in the woods; and the resort was miles away.

Please don't hurt me; please be kind.

I mumbled this like an idiot to myself as I sat there with my head between my legs, rocking back and forth…I was just kind of over all this. And it started since seeing the trippy tree. I didn't have a lick of fight in me left…And I hope I wouldn't need to.

"Why were his eyes like that, that red color?"

Another wave of fear ran through me again.

He looked at me with pity, like he was unsure how to answer.

"You won't see him again, he's long gone. And he won't be coming back."

I got the courage to take a little sideways glance. His eyes weren't anything I remembered when I saw them at the lake. Instead of scary, they were more striking, attractive, even. But still weird. They were icy grey in color mixed in with some orange. Kinda hard to miss.

Even though common sense and logic told me I still wasn't out of the woods, I felt strangely at ease.

But to be honest, in essence, he was scary. He was strong, that was apparent. And I couldn't help but stare because he was so darn pretty. He had a sharp jawline, and it went on forever along with his chin, perfectly sculpted to suit the rest of his face. God himself took extra time with him.

He looked at me with concern. His eyes shimmering like shiny, grey pools.

"You have nothing to fear with me. But I can't say the same for that scoundrel back there. He better stay clear of this area for the next couple hundred years. If I run into him again, I can't say that he would fare very well."

I couldn't help but smile.

"Scoundrel?"

No one says, *Scoundrel.*

He didn't answer but turned to look at me.

"How have you been?"

What a question, and to ask it to someone you don't really know.

"I'm ok."

Considering all that happened, I was more than ok.

"You do remember me, don't you? Because I remember you."

"Yes," I said shakily. "You were the one, well, swimming."

I guess that was the best word for it.

"Well, before I got sidetracked."

"You mean by seeing me?"

I had so many questions for him. I didn't know which one to ask first. I just couldn't believe I was finally sitting here with *him.*

"You really scared me that night."

He looked puzzled like he was drumming up the best answer.

"Well, I'm sorry for that."

I was relieved. I knew he was real. I knew it.

"What happened to you? I mean, where did you go?"

"I've been wondering about you, too."

"Really? People don't just disappear under the water. And if they do it usually means they've drowned."

"Well, here I am, I didn't drown."

"No kidding."

"I've been watching you."

"Watching me, really? Have you ever heard of just maybe, I don't know, walking to my house and taking a knock on the front door?"

He looked amused.

"It might have been a good start."

But as I said these words, I knew that wasn't quite his style.

"How long have you been watching?"

'I guess in your idea of time, several months."

"But you could have just approached me, like a hello would have been nice."

"Well, it didn't seem all that appropriate."

"How can saying hello be inappropriate? You're kinda irritating."

I couldn't believe the words coming out of my mouth.

"I know, but showing myself puts you in danger. However, I'm afraid you already are."

"How could you put me in danger? Besides, you just saved me. And please, do I even want to know what that thing was?"

He smiled.

"Your instincts are good. But no one should come in contact with those things. Especially humans. But that's what I mean, just me being here attracts more danger, more of them."

"But what was he, or it?"

"Maybe that's for another time."

I looked at him. This was a lot to take in, but I could handle it.

"For one, I'm not supposed to even be here. I got stranded, stayed a little too long, and got distracted in the water. I guess I was a little intrigued why you would be doing that, and I wanted to know more."

I thought about what I was doing.

"Really? My fishing made you stay?"

"Well, yes."

Maybe I wasn't such a smooth fisherman as I thought I was.

"And how would that attract danger?"

"Well, that thing that you came in contact with is because of me. They sensed it. They know I'm here, and probably wanted to come take a look around."

"Why do they even care?"

"Believe me they do, they want to know everything that's going on here. Probably keeping tabs for the higher-ups."

"Higher-ups?"

I felt like I was on my first day at elementary school.

"Well, let's just start with this. Everything changed when I decided to show myself to you on the dock. I was supposed to go back to where I'm from, and I was going to..but, I just couldn't."

"Well, I was wondering if I saw things. Is that what you like to do, torture people?"

I was half serious, and hoping I was wrong.

He looked alarmed at first but realized I was kidding.

"I would never do that. And I'm not at all like that thing you encountered. But there are some things you should know about me."

"Ok, fair enough. What are those things?"

"If I come into your life, I end up changing it, permanently."

"Oh."

"Are you ready for that?"

"You promise?" I said smiling.

He smiled and looked me over with a studied eye. I wondered what he could be thinking. I felt powerless to look away. I wondered if this was all part of his plan, putting me under some lovely little spell of his.

His face turned more serious.

"I would like you to try and do something for me."

"What?"

"If you can help it, please don't go out in the woods around here anymore, at least not by yourself."

After what I saw today that wouldn't be hard.

"I thought you said he wasn't coming back."

"Yes, but that doesn't mean something else wouldn't."

"Something else?"

"Look, I'm afraid it's not as safe around here as you're used to it being."

"I'm starting to figure that one out."

I looked down and forgot that my shirt was torn. And my bra was peeking out in the open.

"I just need a few minutes to get my bearings. Please."

"Yes, of course."

He turned away while I tried buttoning up my shirt.

It was useless.

I thought again about the man with the red eyes, how it felt having his hands groping all over me and then came another wave of nausea. I think I was on the verge of a panic attack, and the more I was ignoring it, the stronger it was coming on. I was so embarrassed. My stomach was in knots as I was trying to take some deep breaths. *I felt like I needed air.* I looked around for a paper bag that I knew wouldn't be around. I felt ridiculous and wanted to leave.

"Just focus on something on the ground, a flower maybe. It will ground you."

I turned toward him. "A flower?"

The thought made me laugh inside. But I still spied some small violets that were not too far away. He placed his hand on my shoulder; it felt warm, and nice.

"I know you saw a lot today."

"Sorry."

"Don't be."

There was something about his voice that was soothing, which was a comfort.

"No, I'm sorry. I wasn't sure if I should have made myself known."

"Well, I'm glad you did. I would have always wondered if you didn't."

I was embarrassed. What has he seen about me? Does he know my family? Who else has he spied on? I had so many questions for him. I quick stole another glance under my arm. I could see his stormy eyes up close. His eyelashes were longer then they needed to be. And his lips had that swelled up pouty look. Perfectly kissable. *Being kissed by him would probably feel like magic.*

Even in my panic attack, I was wondering what it would be like to kiss him. Boy, my perspective was off. I could feel his soft breath on my neck; it was oddly soothing. Nothing about this felt like an intrusion, I didn't mind him being this close, and despite what had happened, I was lucky to run into him finally. Honestly, I didn't know whether to faint from the weight of it all or laugh hysterically.

"Take a few deep breaths ok. You'll start to feel better more quickly."

I was already ok, the uneasiness I had was finally going away. The last thing I wanted to do was faint right there. How weak would that look?

"I don't think you're weak."

"Oh no. Can you read minds, too?"

"Well, kind of."

"Oh great. Look, I need some boundaries here, can you just not do that for right now. It's not right or very fair."

"Ok, done. I won't read your mind."

"How do I believe you?"

He just stared at me with that warm grin on his face.

"I guess you are just gonna have to believe me."

"Fair enough."

"I just can't believe what I saw."

"Well, what could be awry? You only saw a tree come to life. That wasn't meant for your eyes, I'm sorry. I just don't have the patience for that kind of recklessness. Even though I know I put you in danger there, I'm sorry."

"*You* did that to the tree? How?"

"It's not something I can easily explain, not today anyway. Trust me on that one."

"And what was that THING? It's ok; you can give it to me straight. I'm not going to freak out or anything."

He smiled a little.

"If you must know, he's called a distractor."

"Ok, a distractor. What about you? Are you um..supernatural too?"

"I am."

My eyes lit up. This was getting better and better. Man, some days you wake up and just haven't a clue about what's in store. I didn't know which to ask first.

"How can you do that, read people's minds?"

"Well, it's a gift and a curse. I'm sorry, it's impolite for me to do so, I know. It's automatic with me, a defense mechanism, but I realize now that it can be intrusive."

"No, it's ok. I just have so many questions, what is going on around here?"

For the first time, I felt strangely relieved. I always knew there was something off here. And today validated it big time. But I was terrified. What did it all mean? Now what?

He looked at me like he wanted to tell.

"Maybe it's better if you knew. But, I don't know."

"You don't know? Hey, I live here. I have a right to know what's going on around me. If you know something, please tell me."

He took a deep breath.

"Ok, well, nothing is as it seems. Not on the outside at least."

"Well, I could have told you that. I'm not your garden variety girl here. I have special powers of my own."

I wouldn't have dreamed of uttering that sentence to any other living soul on the planet. And even now I still wondered about my special sense. It felt strange talking with someone else about it, and so casually. Like we were discussing the weather.

"I know you do."

"But how? That thing back there knew about me too. Do I have some invisible sign that reads, SHE KNOWS YOUR FUTURE?"

"I know you can't help it. Sorry, but I'm not making fun of you."

"I know, it's just hard to talk about. I've always kept it quiet, you know? It's not something you want to broadcast. And even than it was just something that I *suspected,* nothing confirmed. And now, today of all days, both him and you know by just looking at me."

"I can imagine it would be overwhelming."

"Well, you have no idea."

He gave me sort of a pity look then. I wanted to know everything about him. Where he came from, what he thought about, who his parents are etc...

"Maybe you can predict my death."

He said that with a smirk.

"Are you making fun of me?"

"I'm just having a little fun."

"Don't ever joke about your death. I don't think it's funny."

"Ok."

"Look, it's not something I really can control. It just is. And I don't go around telling anybody about it either. I'm not one of those people that gaze into crystal balls. I prefer to keep that to myself."

He laughed at that.

"That would be a little strange."

"Yeah, and this isn't."

He laughed again.

"Look, I will tell you more I promise. But for now, the creature that attacked you, that wasn't random, and I'm sorry for that."

He helped me up and stood before me. He was a lot taller then what I was used to. It was nice to be able to stand up straight and not slump my shoulders.

"He knew I was here. And he was curious. Because I've been here before. And I tend to alter things after I've been to them. That's why I was so reluctant to come back here again."

"But you did."

I felt that electric current run through us again as he took my hand. It felt perfect to hold it. A couple of strands of hair fell into my face. And without missing a beat, he carefully tucked them back behind my ear. His hands were careful, his fingers exquisitely long.

I didn't want him to leave.

"I'm sorry, but I have to go."

My heart dropped.

"Already? But I don't even know who you are."

I felt a little mad. The last thing I wanted him to do was to see him walk away. I felt like the smothering girlfriend that never was. And I didn't want to be that way at all. It just felt right being in his presence. And I could tell I was developing some feelings for him. Someone that I didn't even really know.

But I knew enough.

How in the world can I be attracted to an alien of all things? How does it work? Are we even compatible?

My mind was spinning, and I felt like I had woken up from a coma. For once I was experiencing life as how it should be experienced. I saw things I knew were already there. But now it felt like all that would be disappearing again along with him. I didn't want him to go.

"We should meet again. We can meet right here if you want."

"When?"

"How about tomorrow?"

I shook my head yes. I agreed to a meeting. I would be seeing him again for sure. This would be good.

"Ok, tomorrow. Now get back to your house, your parents will start to worry. It's already late."

I tried thinking of what I had to do; it would be change over day. Nothing more than having to clean up the usual stuff. Thank God it was summertime, and I didn't have to worry about being gone all day at school.

It felt funny talking to him about a meeting. Like we were doing something terrible.

"What time do you want to meet?"

I hoped I wasn't boring him.

"Not possible."

I felt flush.

"You're doing it again, aren't you?"

"I'm sorry. Just come into the woods when you're ready, and I will be here, waiting."

"Hey, wait. What's your name? I don't even know your name!"

"Aaron."

He gave me a quick smile. I returned it, and my face was redder for it. I bent down to gather myself together, and when I looked up, he was already gone.

This was frustrating. Where could he have moved on to so quickly?

"Hey, where'd you go?" I yelled out in the woods.

Why did he have to move so fast?

No reply. All I could hear was the distance shriek of birds. Yeah, I can imagine that the birds around here would be pretty riled up. I could tell he was already far away, but the things around me now felt different, charged.

Like he uncovered a veil, and I was seeing things how they were meant to be seen.

But all I could hear was the same phrase echo over and over in my head.

I'll meet with you tomorrow. And I promise it will be a much longer visit and under much better circumstances. Now start walking home before your parents start to worry.

Sleep well, Brooke.

Sleep well, Brooke. I liked the way he said my name. I liked the way he hesitated before saying it. I didn't know where it was coming from and how I could be hearing it in my head like that, but I did. I wondered if he could still read my mind now that he was gone.

As I found the familiar path past the tree farm, I could see the outline of our home. I couldn't hear anything from him anymore. Aaron assured me the distractor wouldn't be back, but now I wasn't so sure. I shuddered to think of where it was right now, this very minute. Where would something like that come from? I wanted to know. Then I would be sure to go in the opposite direction.

Now it was time to figure out what I was going to say to mom so I could sneak away for a few hours tomorrow. I would have to get all my chores done first thing. I was going over in my mind all the things that I would have to do, clean the pool, clean the game room, bail out the boats... When I could start to see the outline of home, I smiled.

I ran as fast as I could. And I couldn't get there soon enough.

As soon as I opened the door, I saw Mom bending down at the oven checking on the pot roast. Its mouthwatering smell filtered throughout the house, reminding me how hungry I was. After coming back to the safety of home, I stood there and looked out of our window that overlooked the lake, somewhat in a daze. Did all that just happen? I went over all the events in the past hour, and it just didn't seem possible.

What was I going to do?

How can I live with this kind of secret?

I was glad for our house, and the lock on the door. I was happy to have some time away from those woods, even though it was still close by.

It was exciting knowing he was out there somewhere. I wondered already what he was doing, where he was going. Was he in the water? Is that how he always traveled? Where was he watching me all those months?

I wondered if he was still thinking about me.

I had a million questions, and I was so excited I could barely think straight.

The sun was setting. It was pretty, except now everything seemed more edgy, dangerous.

Things in my life were going to be a little different now.

And I have just been given a little taste of it.

A NEW NORMAL

I woke up with a start. My mouth was bone dry and my stomach growled like I hadn't eaten in a week. I sat up in bed a little too quickly and was reminded of the cut on my leg. I ran my hand over it. It was sore and bumpy. I would need to clean it soon, but I would live.

I made a mental note to get some Neosporin on it. Mom always had it in the house. As long as Patti wasn't sniffing around while I got it, I would be fine. She could put two and two together quicker than anyone. The less she knew about what happened yesterday, the better.

As I got up, I noticed I hadn't bothered changing clothes from the night before; I had been too tired. I was achy and sore, but also a little exhilarated. I could feel fresh scratches scattered about on my arms and legs. And a few bruises had cropped up overnight. I would have to think up a reason for that.

I could feel something in me had profoundly changed. Like I was let in on a secret that no one else knew anything about. I looked around the room. Nothing in appearance looked outwardly different. My bed was still the same… my annoying, uneven desk was still there in the corner. Evidence of my short-lived swimming career hung on my bulletin board. Three ribbons that were starting to shrivel up at the ends. Things in my room were still the same and where I left them.

From now on I was going to start questioning the details. And for the oddest reason, the most unlikely person came to mind. The girl that was currently staying in cabin 4. The one whom I thought had a few screws loose, and that was being nice about it.

Penny was different, that was for sure, and yesterday I wouldn't have given two hoots about her. But now she was someone I really wanted to talk to. Why? For some reason, I thought that she could give me some answers. But from what has transpired in the last 24 I couldn't even fathom. How would I begin?

It was unsettling to me that creepy things were running about in our woods. Apparently, the bad ones can fly, have freaky looking eyes, and have a visceral distaste for anything human. And they also have a fondness for whiskey. And I was going to find out why. If that meant befriending the strangest girl I knew, so be it. Would she have answers for me? I didn't know why, but I thought she might.

Last week I remembered her walking up from one of our docks. I checked the register and saw that her family would be staying for two weeks. She was dressed like Laura Ingalls Wilder. Her face had an old-world quality about it. What should have been youthful happiness instead was weariness and worry. Too much stress for a girl of her age.

Her long hair was blowing about in the wind right in step with her billowy skirt. She was walking up our pebbled driveway that crisscrossed through the heart of our resort. She had been looking all around her and up at the sky quite nervously. She looked like she was afraid that the sky was falling.

I got in the shower and stood under the hot water as long as I could stand it. It felt good to wash off the day before. As I lathered up my hair, I could still see the image of the creep with the dead red eyes. A face like that wasn't something you could easily forget.

Despite standing under hot water, I was chilled. I tried to forget everything while I let the hot water relax my muscles. I pictured Aaron with his soft eyes. I could have stayed under there for hours, my little private hideaway.

The bathroom was hot and misty as I tiptoed out and dried off with one of our nicer, fluffy towels. It was amazing what a perfect shower could do, and I was thankful for it. This would help me get into the right frame of mind to figure out how I was going to deal with things now.

I put on a fresh pair of shorts and my favorite cotton tee and went downstairs. My legs were shaky, but I tried to look as normal as possible as I poured myself a bowl of Frosted Flakes. But normal was the last thing I was feeling. I was reminded of how hungry I was, and couldn't seem to shovel it in fast enough.

"What's up with you?"

I could feel Patti's eyes boring into me. Unfortunately, she was on her game. In another minute she would be nit picking me with endless questions about yesterday. She always had an eye for detail. She would make a good FBI agent one day.

"Just hungry," I said in between bites.

"No duh. But hello, it's not going anywhere, we have a whole box."

I rolled my eyes at her. There was no way I could say anything about what happened. Of course, I wouldn't, I did not want anyone in my family to become vulnerable. As long as I knew they were safe, I wouldn't be telling them.

I was going to have to figure out a way to dodge her questions. The less she knew, the better. My mom had her back to me, she was busy cleaning out the fridge. She had most everything out and sitting on top of the table. Drops of condensation were already forming on it. She was trying to clean out all the junk that had been sitting in the bottom of the drawers. Sometimes the resort took precedence over household chores.

"You were gone for a long time yesterday. Where'd you go?"

Patti looked up and stared right at me.

"Oh, just walking around in the woods, you're always telling me to 'go outside.'"

"Well, you could have brought a bucket with you. The berries are perfect now."

"I know I saw them. I'll pick some today."

"Listen, I need to talk to you. Your father and I would rather you not wander around in the woods anymore."

"Why?"

I tried sounding as innocent as I could.

"He caught a few guys trying to cut down some of our trees across the road yesterday."

"Oh."

"He was going to call the DNR, but when he started talking to them, they weren't making too much sense. Apparently, something scared them. Anyway, they went straight back to their cabin, packed up and left. Just don't go out there until we figure out what's going on, ok?"

She sounded pretty nervous.

I turned around.

"What did they see?"

"I don't know quite what they saw; they didn't want to talk about it. But they did cut their vacation short, which is unusual. I think maybe they had a little too much to drink at Margie's and probably saw a bear or something. Just packed up their things, and left."

"Really? Huh."

"I'm hoping their out of state check clears the bank, but I'm not counting on it. Just don't go wandering out too far, ok?"

"Alright."

I was trying to figure out how I was going to get time away to meet up with Aaron. It was still hard to make sense of what happened. Despite seeing it with my own eyes, I still had a hard time believing myself. It still felt like a dream. And meanwhile, my frosted flakes were getting soggier by the minute.

"Where did you get those bruises?"

Patti grabbed my arm and tried turning it over.

"I just fell. No big deal."

"But what were you doing?"

"I don't know, walking around."

I made a mental note of having to get rid of the torn shirt from the day before. I didn't want to have to explain the big rip and torn off buttons, which my mom would undoubtedly discover if I left it in there. I was a terrible liar as it was.

"Just watch your step on these grounds ok? There are lots of ways to get hurt."

"I will, Mom."

My mind was busy as I cleaned up the table and put the dishes in the sink. I was going to have to help her with laundry later which I wasn't looking forward to at all. It was right up there with having to go to the front of the room and talk in front of everyone in speech class. Well, it was surely better than that, but not by much.

Our laundry house on the resort was located right in the middle of all the cabins. It was where mom and I did all the bedding on the resort grounds. It was a tiny little thing, like a very small cabin. I don't even know how they managed to get two washing machines in it. And the door always took several tugs to get open.

The doorway was uneven, and a bit rotten, and always swelled up when we had a good rain. It always required a good tug to get it open. The air was always thick and smelled of earth and rain. There were little uneven wooden shelves on both sides of the walls. The area to wash in was so narrow it made you feel claustrophobic, even if you weren't prone to those things.

At best it could fit two people, and that was pushing it. The shelves were always packed with containers of Tide and Gain and dryer sheets and clothespins. All the corners had been invaded by spider webs, made by huge Wolf spiders. Some of the biggest I've ever seen.

As I was helping mom unload loads of sheets from the wash, I couldn't help but let my mind drift a little. She would cringe if she ever knew what happened. But she would never know because I would never be telling her. I could never tell anybody.

And how long has this been going on? Was their kind living and breathing among us the whole time and I'm just now finding out about it? How many other people know? Does June? Does Margie? Are there people in Neelsville that know already? And

how do you go about resuming daily life without continually looking over your shoulder? I shudder to think if Mr. Red Eyes ever
found me again.

It took forever to finish my chores. And to top it off, I had to
help with dinner, and now there was barely any light left in the
day. I was out of patience and itching for the right excuse to slip
away. I never did get a chance to find Penny. I looked around, but
she hadn't been at her cabin all day. Her dad wasn't either. I did
notice that their boat was gone, so I figured maybe they were just
out fishing for the day.

It was already sunset, and no matter how bad I wanted to see
Aaron again I wasn't looking forward to venturing off by myself.
Let alone out in the woods. I had enough of an adventure the other
day. I wondered why he couldn't just come to me. Lulling this over
in my head I decided that I had to see him. And that won over.

Curiosity killed the cat.

As soon as everyone was settled in and had gone to bed, I was
lying on top of my bed wide awake staring up at the tile lines of my
ceiling. It could have been noon to me. My heart thumped loudly
in my chest as I slowly opened my window to the outside world.
I quick climbed through and made the little jump to the ground.
I looked up at the dark sky and noticed that there was no moon.

Great.

Mr. Red Eyes could use that to his advantage for sure. I couldn't
believe I was doing this knowing that he could be out there somewhere, lurking about amongst the trees. I would have to do a little
bit of walking before I even passed the main light which overlooked
the road across from the woods. What if Red Eyes was just waiting
for me to come out?

But he said he wouldn't come here again.

But that was Aaron's words, not his. How could Aaron know that? I mean, how could he be so sure? I wondered where all those creatures ended up going? Some dark, faraway land somewhere? What if they liked being here instead?

I could start to see a few stars as I made my way to the middle of the resort. That was a comfort, but a small one. All the cabins and the bushes next to them looked like dark, ominous clumps. It felt like anything could just jump out in front of me. I was glancing back every two seconds. I wanted to run back to the house every step of the way, but wanting to see Aaron won over.

As I could see my house getting farther and farther away, I was starting to lose some of my courage. I stopped and looked around. I was afraid of what might be hiding near me. It was a long walk back to the house already. As I stood, I felt a warm breeze run itself through the trees of the forest, rustling the leaves. This wasn't making things easier.

I looked around and stood at the forest edge. This was quite dumb. I should just go home.

"Over here."

My head snapped in the direction of his voice.

"Where? I can't see you."

"You'll see me."

I looked in each direction, I couldn't really see anything. I scanned the woods again and saw what looked to be a pair of eyes far off into the woods.

"Just follow my voice."

Gladly, I thought.

"Just come further in, you'll see me."

I've already seen you.

I carefully did as he asked, but with caution. I didn't want to step on anything or come across anything. I took the overgrown path Patti and I had made the previous year. I remember it took us forever to try and finish last summer. Hours of digging up roots in the hot sun, now it was overgrown again. All that work for nothing. But it was a comfort to walk through it as I got to the middle of the meadow.

I could start to see more of his outline. Just seeing his shadow there made my heart race.

I knew it was him but still got the hairs on my neck standing on ends.

"Don't be scared." He said.

Yeah, right.

His voice was soft and soothing. But all you had to do was just look at him to see otherwise. He looked dangerous. He did save me once, but did that mean I could trust him?

"You can. And next time you see me, you won't be as alarmed."

I stopped dead in my tracks.

"Please, I don't know if I can handle you hearing everything that I think. That's not exactly fair ground here. You mind turning it off?"

I felt nervous asking him this, but I couldn't help it.

"That's fair. Will do."

"So, you turned your ability off now? You can't hear my thoughts?"

"Yes, and I'll make sure to do that from now on."

"That would be great. But how do I know you're not giving me a line?"

He stood there grinning, looking too beautiful to be real. He took a few careful steps closer and whispered in my ear.

"You'll just have to trust me."

"Ok. But I have my ways of finding out."

"I don't doubt that you do. Your thoughts will be completely to yourself for this and every meeting."

"Is this what this is, a meeting?"

A meeting, out in the woods.

I was only a couple feet in front of him now, and it was intimidating. He was gorgeous, no doubt about it. Not that it made him any less scary, but to be honest, it did help. Well, that little bit of frightening walk to get to him was well worth it. His eyes did not have that odd cast to him anymore. It didn't seem fair that he could be more beautiful than me.

"I was afraid you wouldn't want to see me again."

"Really? Um, no. I meant what I said. How could I not want to see you?"

He smiled again. *Oh boy.*

"Well, considering everything that happened yesterday, that might have been a deterrent."

"Well, I don't scare that easily."

"No, you don't."

I turned my attention to my Converse sneakers.

"I would have been here sooner, but it was hard to get away today."

"You don't have to apologize to me, I understand."

So many questions, but where to begin? He seemed to sense this.

"How about a walk?" he asked.

Perfect.

"Whatever you like."

"Walking along the road is fine. And I promise nothing is going to hurt you as long as I'm here."

Walking felt safer than standing with him in the woods. Maybe I was over thinking it, but I wasn't entirely sure about him. He had turned up every emotion on me, and it took some getting used to.

We walked down the road. There was a period of silence; I just didn't know what to say to him first. But the more we walked, the more relaxed I became. Pony road was practically a ghost town in the evening, so we weren't going to be bothered, which I was glad.

"So, you've been watching me, huh?"

He smiled and looked down.

"I'm sorry about that. Yes, you are somewhat of a distraction I'm afraid."

He was hard to look away from. He looked like some mythical Greek God. A Greek God in a pair of Levi's. I wondered where the heck he got his clothes. Because in that way, he looked normal. I could see the strength of his arms. I tried to focus on something else. I noticed that he had been holding something in his hand and he was popping it in his mouth like candy.

"These are wonderful."

He had a handful of blackberries.

"Yeah, they're pretty good."

"Did you want some?"

"Sure."

I cupped my hand towards him, and he dropped a few in my palm. Our fingers touched briefly, and I felt that electric current again.

"Ok, Aaron. Where exactly are you from?"

"Cutting to the chase, aren't we?"

"Yeah, I guess so. But we both know you are not from here."

"What makes you say that?"

Mr. Easy on the eyes liked messing with me. That was ok, I could deal with that.

"Well, we could start with your freaky looking eyes."

"What? These ole things?"

His eyes looked mischievous in the moonlight. He was charming, but just the same I preferred that he didn't make them glow.

"But you don't have to turn on the glow or whatever you call it, it just scares me a little."

"No glow. I can do that."

"And your clothes? They're just like ours."

"Well, we do know how to blend in, and, we do have our resources."

"But he didn't."

Mr. Red Eyes was very different. His dress was something out of a different couple centuries.

"The way they dress isn't of particular importance. They know they can manipulate anyone, so they don't bother hiding anything."

"Where are they from?"

"Like me, he's from out of town."

"Gee, that narrows it down."

He stopped.

"Sorry, I just have to be careful what I tell you."

"I know, I just want to know. This is where I live, and it's tough knowing that this stuff is going on and I'm in the dark about it."

"Well, I think you've already figured it out, that I'm not like you."

Of course, I knew that the first day I saw him. But it wasn't like he was complete science fiction either; he had many human traits, like talking, dressing, thinking as we do.

"I'm not...a human."

He almost whispered the last two words, as if embarrassed.

"I know, but what are you then?"

"I don't know, I guess your kind would consider me; an alien."

This made sense, but scary to hear out loud.

"You mean different planet and everything?"

He didn't hesitate.

"Yes."

"I look human. And have the same characteristics, but I can assure you, I am very much not."

I stopped in my tracks.

"How did you get here?"

I knew he had otherworldly strengths. That was apparent after yesterday.

"And I'm putting you and your family in danger with everything I'm telling you. Do you really want that?"

"But why did you agree to meet then?"

I watched as his eyes took a sad tone.

"Because I wanted to see you again. I'm sorry. Even if it means putting you in danger. I guess I was willing to take that chance. Again, I'm sorry."

"No, don't be. I wanted to see you again, too."

"Really?"

I shook my head.

"Well good."

"But how would it put me in danger? I think knowing would be better, wouldn't it?"

"Unfortunately, it's better if you don't know."

"Why?"

"Well, for instance, that thing that was groping you, yesterday. That was not at all close to being human."

"No offense, Aaron, but I figured that one out."

He smirked at that one, but his voice took a serious tone.

"That was a distractor."

"Distractor?"

"They're a lot more frequent then they used to be. And they can easily blend in with other parts of society. Like us. And they have powers of their own. Unfortunately, when you come in contact with one of them, like me, they can change the course of anything. They arrive on malice, causing chaos. But they do have one downfall, and that is they get bored. And they get distracted themselves, quite easily in fact. And they don't like to stay in one place for too long."

"Is there more of them?"

"Quite a few more."

"But where do they live?"

"With us, with you, in the cities, in the countryside. Unfortunately, they're all over the place. More in some towns then others. They are inherently evil. And they permeate everywhere. They are put in place to distract, to make humans do things they wouldn't normally do. They can do so many things, Brooke. They can mess with time, they can control the weak, they can take people off their original born path."

"Born path?"

"They don't like it when people are happy. It makes them jealous; they hate it in fact. Because they are miserable, they want to make everybody else feel the same. And believe me, they have endless ways of doing it."

I thought about this.

"Can they really cause accidents?"

"They do it all the time."

"Like car accidents?"

"Natural disasters, earthquakes, floods, accidents, and more. And they don't stop."

"Aren't those things caused by weather?"

"Yes, some are, and some are not."

"Isn't life already chaotic?"

"Believe me, it could get a lot worse."

"But where do they come from?"

"We're not quite sure, or even when but we just know that they are. And they come in a multitude of forms."

"But how did they get here?"

"Same way we did, we think, but we don't know for sure. But in twenty years' time or so, the earth here is going to get worse. They can change form. They inhabit inanimate objects. Your kind will be fixated and not be able to do anything but use these devices. And it's meant to distract you. It's meant to give you illness, cause accidents, break down relationships, to fragment families, to keep you scattered, to lose focus. Nothing is sacred. The fundamental principle of communication will be shattered. All real meaning just lost."

None of this made much sense to me.

"But how would you know what is happening twenty years from now?"

He rubbed the front of his head.

"I'm sorry, I shouldn't have told you all this. It's a lot to take in, and I'm afraid I've already told you way too much."

"No, I want to know."

"It makes me sick."

"What makes you sick?"

He looked off into the distance.

"The reason that thing went after you, is because of me."

"Because of you? Why would that matter? Why would it care?"

"Because we're all supernatural Brooke. I'm not supposed to be here, not really."

"But then, how are you here?"

"It's a long story."

I didn't intend to grab his arm, but I did. I felt that electricity between us again, even though it was brief.

He certainly was different. He moved like no one I had ever seen before, and despite this, he was careful in his way of moving. As if he was always holding back.

"Listen, can I ask you something?"

"Sure."

"How long have you lived here?"

"Unfortunately, all my life."

I thought about how life could slow down too much for my liking sometimes. This seemed to make up for it all.

"It's beautiful here, Brooke. You should know that. And you're lucky to live here in the middle of all these trees and lakes."

"I know."

We walked side by side. He smelled like the woods after a good rain. When I was with him, he made everything ugly go away. And that was the God's honest truth.

"How long have you been watching me?"

"A few months."

I was stunned.

"Really? But I never saw you at all."

"Well, that was the idea."

I stopped in my tracks.

"Do you realize I've been thinking and wondering about you in the past year? I thought I would never see you again."

"I'm sorry. I almost thought about not coming back. I just didn't think it would be safe to reveal myself."

He watched me closely.

I looked up at the sky. I wondered how nice it would be to watch the stars with him. I could probably do that for hours.

"Can you hear everything that I think?"

"Mostly things that you feel strongly about. But yeah, pretty much. But like I said, for this meeting, I turned it off."

I couldn't help but smile. This was odd.

As we walked ahead, we could hear signs of nightlife in the woods, crickets, frogs, everything.

"When I saw you that night, it was like everything had stopped."

"I know, I did that. I wasn't sure what you were doing at first."

"Me? I was fishing. What the heck were you doing?"

"I was swimming."

"Would you teach me to fish sometime?"

That seemed funny that he would ask ME how to fish. Especially since he looked like he could very well manage that on his own, without the crude tool like a fishing pole. I smiled.

"You've never seen anyone fish?"

"Oh, I have, but I never really paid much attention to it. You caught my eye, however."

He reached out and grazed my cheek with his long fingers.

"Your cheek is so soft."

"Where are you from?"

"Can I just say for now, that I live far away?"

"I guess. But what's the big secret, you know where I live."

"True. Maybe someday I could take you there. But I would have to get permission first."

Permission from whom?? Baby steps. That topic would have to be for another time.

"Why are there strange things in the woods?"

"Let's start with this. I'll tell you why I'm here. We're here to test your planet, the waters, the animals. To see if maybe they might be compatible in our lands."

Heart is thumping loudly in the chest.

"How old are you?"

"Too old in human terms."

"This is crazy."

"I've come to help. To see what I can do."

"Why?"

"Something is coming to your planet."

"The distractors?"

"Yes, but they are just part of them. There's a certain race that despises everything here on earth. And they could care less about humans."

I listened in horror. I couldn't believe my ears. And couldn't believe he was trusting me with it.

"And they're going to come, they're going to come in droves, and I can't emphasize that enough. I just wanted to let you know, I felt like I needed you to know. I couldn't bare you not knowing."

I stood and listened to what he was saying. I heard, but I could not believe what he was saying to me. It was like he was telling me something out of a fairy tale.

Times a million.

"What does this mean for us, then?"

"It means you need to figure out a way to defeat them. Because they will be coming, we just don't know when, but it's inevitable."

"So, what are we supposed to do? Are we doomed?"

"We're trying to help with that."

"What do you mean we?"

"Our kind."

"I have a few gifts, I guess you would call them. I can see things in addition to reading minds. My brother is better at seeing the future than I can. But people that know of me, their future gets skewed, changed."

"You have a brother?"

I couldn't imagine what he would look like. If it was anything like Aaron, well there was another lucky girl out there.

"How can you change futures?"

I looked at him with awe. He evidently was changing mine.

"I wasn't supposed to stay in this area for too long, but I wanted to come back. I guess I wanted to see if you were for real."

"Really?"

"You've got an unusual light around you. You pull the good things in. But you can also pull people in who may not be very savory, I'm afraid. I put myself in that category."

"Well, I wouldn't."

He smiled and said nothing more. It was peaceful walking with him. I felt safe despite all the talk of alien beings, special powers, and the world being at war with them. And I know he was big time playing down his ability and strengths.

"Your pretty strong, aren't you? I mean you pulled that guy off me like he was a piece of lint."

"What is lint?"

"Well, it's something you can find in the dryer."

"I had to act; I didn't want him to go farther with you."

"Well, thank you."

"Could I ask something of you, if I may?"

He's reading my thoughts once again. Great.

"You have the advantage of reading my mind, that isn't fair."

"The world has never been fair. Sorry, I said I wouldn't read your mind at this meeting. I stopped."

"Just like that?"

"Yep."

"How do I know you're not fooling with me?"

"Guess you'll have to trust me." He revealed a sly grin.

I stood there in his presence. Scared to do anything more. Afraid of making the wrong move.

Afraid he will. Afraid he won't. In a way, he reminded me of an animal, somewhat tamed but still wild. Like if I made one false move....

I froze as he brought his hands up and gently grazed both sides of my cheek with his thumbs.

That was nice. And his touch was so gentle. So different compared to how he looked. As long as his eyes didn't do that crazy thing again. That would make me stop in my tracks. I hoped then that he would kiss me.

"Your cheek is so soft," he said again, staring at me.

He grazed it with his thumb while staring at me. It was a piercing come-hither stare, and almost impossible to stare back. I sure hoped he wasn't reading my mind because right now I would want to die.

"Brooke, I thought that maybe you would like a kiss. Is that what you want?"

"Um, yes!"

Is he for real? I could kiss him for days.

It would be quite lovely to kiss him. I was sure of that. Even though I never experienced what a good kiss was. I didn't count the sloppy, wet one I received from Gregg Stanley. We were playing spin the bottle, and I was the lucky girl. It was a forced thing, and too wet for my liking and something I'd rather not repeat. Surely all kisses weren't like that.

I stood there while his lips found mine. They weren't cold, or alien-like at all. They were just, warm.

"You're very tempting," he said.

It was an odd thing to hear someone say that, but also sweet. I could feel him lingering beside my neck.

"Aaron, it's ok," I whispered.

"You are lovely." He said this as he started kissing my neck.

"I'm sorry," I said out of breath. I needed a few minutes, I really did.

"No, don't be sorry. I didn't mean to do that."

"Yeah, you did. But I wanted you to."

"You shouldn't initiate things like that with me."

Me? What was he saying? I was confused.

"I thought you wanted to kiss me. Sorry, I disappointed you."

"No, no, you didn't disappoint. I just don't want to hurt you."

"How can you hurt me?"

"Well, I easily could have you know. Humans are extremely fragile compared to us."

"Aaron, I don't care what you are. But I do know everything changed after I saw you at the lake. I know you're different. And I know that you are strong, you have certain powers. It's ok."

"I thought about you a lot during the last twelve months. They have been some of the longest months of my life."

"Really?" I had too much hope in my voice.

"I wondered about the girl with the fishing pole. Yes, you're right. I watched you. And I am sorry for that."

I was kind of angry with him. The whole time I've been going on with life, trying to forget what I saw, him, getting on with school. He had been there the entire time, spying on me. That explains the prickly sensation that I could never seem to shake.

"You know in my world that's called stalking."

"You need to know that every time I make myself known to you, I'm altering your path, in fact, I'm doing it right now. This is only going to attract more of them."

"But why do they even care?"

"Because that's what they do, Brooke. They like to create havoc. But if no one knows, they can't be revealed. But I opened the door on that one."

He looked exasperated. He sat down on a nearby rock. He held his head in his hands, which made him look lovingly innocent.

He didn't move. Just sat on the rock, looking like a statue.

I wanted more from him; I didn't have the patience for waiting anymore.

"Where do you come from?"

"I told you, far away from here."

"Did you fly?"

He stifled a loud chuckle.

I don't know why I asked that.

"What's so funny?"

"We can't unless you have another couple hundred years."

His lovely grin was hard to watch. It made me not want to stay mad at him.

I couldn't help myself. I stood there, wanting him to do more. I didn't know how to initiate it. But he indeed read my mind and was one step ahead of me. In one quick motion he got up from the rock, and with a steady hand, he gently led me to the ground. Before I could do anything, he was on top of me.

"Is this what you want? Me here having my way with you."

He looked down at me, and his eyes had that glare to them. It was that scary glow, both menacing and lovely at the same time. He held my wrists down on the ground as if I were his prey. Just like Mr. Red Eyes.

But this was different. This didn't feel like a violation.

Before I could think of what he would do, he was off me in a flash, and already several feet away. I was still sitting on the ground. The quickness with the way he moved was more than a little disconcerting.

"How do you DO that?"

I stared at him while he watched me.

"How could you watch me for an entire year, and not bother coming out to say hello? Not one time. And now you're telling me that I'm driving you crazy. Well, how about this. YOU'RE crazy with all this double talk of yours. If you came back to see me, then you need to start giving me some answers. Believe me, I'm a big girl, I think I can handle it."

"You're more aware of signs. You realize that, don't you?" he asked.

I did have a propensity for things around me, like a sixth sense for things. But now my senses felt utterly awaken. No, I could never go back to pretending everything was just black and white, with no grey. Because this indeed was the magical grey.

"Distractors know that, too. And they want someone like you on their side."

He touched my arm. With his hand, he gave me a reassuring caress.

"Your arm smells delicious. I could take a bite of it right here."

I stopped. Dear God, I hoped he was kidding.

He laughed.

"I'm sorry, wrong choice of words. You should know I would never really do that. I would never harm you. But I think you know that already, don't you?"

"I do, I think. But your charms can only go so far."

I lied. His charms got probably about as far as I wanted them to. He was the second guy I've ever kissed. Well, technically he was an alien. Ok, my first alien kiss.

The thought of him leaving made me sick. I wanted him to kiss me again. Just one more time.

"Aaron, would you…

Before I got the rest of my words out, there he was at my side. He had cupped my face with his hands and stared in my face. He had given me the softest kiss. I kissed him back. Everything else around us just faded into the background. It was just him and me, and this electricity that I hoped would never end.

I wished he could come back with me. Back to the calmness of my bedroom, back to my pretty lace curtains covered in soft purple flowers. Back to safety and rules and being happy with just the every day.

I couldn't believe how strong my feelings were for this man I didn't know; I mean not entirely. Or should I say, alien? Of course, leave it to me to fall in love for the first time with something that wasn't human.

I needed time away from his hungry eyes and thoughts. I didn't trust myself around him for very long.

"I think I need some time."

"I understand." He said. He said he understood, but he still looked like I punched him in the gut. It made me feel like I was the bad one. God, I hated that. I hated how he was making me feel. He was changing my world alright.

"I think I need to go home."

"Ok."

"You are not leaving, right? Please promise me that."

"As long as you want me here. I can stay here for a little while."

"What's a little while?"

He smiled.

"It's plenty of time, believe me."

"Good. But where do I find you?"

"We can meet at night. And out in the woods, if that's ok. It's more secret there."

"Ok. I have to go home now."

I didn't want to, but it felt like the right thing to do. Before both of us did something that we would end up regretting. This was crazy, but I was scared of my feelings. Alien or not, this was more than some crush.

THE PICNIC

*Y*ou could tell that it was 4th of July weekend in Neelsville. The local grocery, Neelson's was packed. Everyone in town was getting stocked up on the weekend essentials of beer, burgers, brats, and fireworks.

Anticipation filled the air along with an early start of the fireworks. People were looking forward to celebrating the long weekend. This meant my parents were going to be busy with the annual summer picnic that they usually have at their resort. Everyone who stayed there was invited, along with several neighbors on either side of the resort and along Pony Road. Which meant a lot of food.

My dad wasn't shy about asking the butcher at Neelson's for specific cuts of meat so he would get the best cuts at the best price. And my mom was quite the cook. She had the gift of being able to whip something up that could feed fifty people, easy.

We were busy pushing all the picnic tables' together right along the lake, so everyone would have a place to sit and eat. Then afterward, people could either go for a swim in the pool or stay a while and gather around my dad while he got out the guitar.

The party would be in full-swing shortly. I walked around the table that was filled with everything scrumptious. Homemade baked beans with bacon, a couple of different salads with little marshmallows in it, and dozens of grilled corn on the cob, bratwursts, sauerkraut, and plates of barbecued chicken. All just sitting in bowls waiting for us to dig in.

Lyle and Cassie were there sitting down at the corner of the picnic table. Her friend Ethel was sitting close by. They were like two peas in a pod. The Johnson's were there, along with extended family members that I didn't know. Guy and his girlfriend were there. Of course, she was looking radiant as ever.

Margie was there minus her two dogs. Still looking like a Dr. Seuss character, she could never disappoint. She looked like she couldn't decide what to eat first on her plate. It was a busy, fun atmosphere. I grabbed a paper plate and loaded up on some of the goodies before me.

"So, I guess you are pretty hungry."

It was Guy. Standing there being his charming self. I still liked him, that was for sure, but I noticed that my feelings for him were starting to shift. Or maybe he was different, somehow. I don't know, maybe it was when I kissed Aaron. Who knows, but something felt different. I just didn't know what it was.

"It is pretty good. Where's Lisa? Isn't she eating?"

"She only eats vegetarian type stuff."

I just shook my head.

"God forbid she should eat a hot dog."

He smirked.

"She's not feeling well."

"Oh, I'm sorry."

I didn't know how to really respond to that. I was still mulling over what happened in the past couple of days. And figuring out how to process all the information that I had been given. Aaron and I met a few more times over the last couple of days. But it was only at night, and for only twenty minutes or so, and it was never enough. We both decided it would just be easier that way so no one else would see us and ask more questions.

What would anybody do? It's not like I could take the info to the police or the FBI. I would be the laughing stock of the town. And I would probably have to end up going to see a psychiatrist. Why would I want any of that breathing down my neck?

I didn't. So, I just pretended that everything was normal.

"You seem different." Guy said.

"Well, maybe I am."

He gave me a strange once over. Maybe he noticed something different in me, I could feel it.

"Feel like going for a swim later?" he asked.

"Yeah sure." I always liked going for a swim.

I said this casually as I walked away. I just didn't feel like dealing with Guy today. I found a seat next to Patti, who was staring at her plate, busy swirling a cherry tomato through her Italian dressing.

"Hey, some guy was asking for you."

I perked up.

"Who?"

"He's over at the food table. Not bad looking, either."

I about snapped my neck trying to turn my head around fast enough. And sure enough, there he was. Mr. Grey-eyed alien. He was normal as ever, though. If you called a Greek God as being normal.

I saw that he had already helped himself to a plate of food. Inside, I panicked a little.

WHAT WAS HE DOING? WHAT IF PEOPLE FOUND OUT ABOUT HIM?

What would people do if he knew what he was? But, I did need to give him some credit. He wasn't going to spill the beans on himself. And he had a way of adapting to situations. I had to trust it. I watched cautiously as he came toward me with a smug grin on his face. He sat down right next to Patti and me.

"Ok, besides the obvious, what are you doing here?"

"Well I'm getting some food, and I'm hungry. Looking after you isn't easy after all."

This sounded strange to me. He seemed like he would be above eating food. But he did eat berries the other day...

I whispered in his ear.

"Please do not start reading my mind either, it's very annoying."

"Ok."

"So how do I know you are not?"

In between bites of salad, "Guess you'll have to trust me."

Inside I still had anxiety about people finding out. I just couldn't wipe out that worry. He turned to me softly just then.

"Give me a little credit here. What is the phrase you guys like to use? I've been around the block."

I couldn't help but smile.

"And they are not gonna notice unless you keep acting the way you do."

I nodded and tried eating. I could see Patti was chomping at the bit waiting for me to do the introducing.

"Aaron, this is my sister Patti."

"Well, how do you do?"

"Great, thanks."

"Well, I guess beauty runs in the family."

She rolled her eyes. She was playing it off, but I knew she was charmed by his words.

Deep down I was glad he was here. Knowing what I knew, it was good that he was around. He just made things, *better*.

"So, where do you stay at?"

"Not far from here."

I watched him as he took a massive bite of a hamburger.

"This is really good," he said in between bites.

He had a whimsical little look in his eye. I think he dug hamburgers.

Patti looked at me like I just said the dumbest thing in the world.

I wanted to laugh, but I had a mouthful. The look on her face was priceless.

"Well, let's get one thing clear. We don't get to eat many hamburgers where I'm from."

He said this while licking his fingers. Boy, I wish he wouldn't do that.

Patti just laughed it off.

"It's just a hamburger."

She thought he was kidding. This was good. The fewer people knew about him, the better. It was amazing how he could blend in. If you count the most good-looking man in the world blending in with us mere mortals, because that's what it felt like.

I could feel Cassie's stare before I even saw her. I could only imagine the sinful thoughts rolling around in that colorful mind of hers. I loved Cassie to death, but one thing that irked me the most was her shameless flirting. I overheard her tell a dirty joke one day at one of my dad's parties. They didn't think I was around, but I was. I could hear her behind my tree. She had one of the loudest voices ever.

I could tell she was patiently waiting to strike. Like a pit viper. Except I wouldn't consider Aaron innocent prey. She was wearing her favorite lipstick; you could have seen those lips a mile away in a snowstorm. She was smoking of course. If your ever inclined to smoke, never go near Cassie because she would make it glamorous and cool. I watched her seductively take a few drags from her cigarette and blow it in Aaron's direction. She was piling it on pretty thick, and I was getting annoyed.

I felt a possessive twinge in me.

I *saw him first.*

Aaron sure seemed to have that magnetic pull.

Saying Aaron was attractive would be a gross understatement. And if we were going to spend any time together, I guess I was going to have to get used to girls ogling, young or old.

Lyle seemed oblivious to any of this. He was busy talking to a few others at the table about fishing. That topic could go around that group for hours. Ethel Haskins came over with her plate of food and plopped herself next to Cassie. Cassie moved over, more than happy to oblige. Ethel was Cassie's shadow. I had to admit, I wondered about them sometimes.

"Well, doll, when you gonna introduce me to this wonderful visitor of ours?"

Aaron kept on eating. I couldn't help but think how he was enjoying all this adoration and attention.

"Cassie Lynn, this is Aaron."

"Well, how do you do?" She said as she extended a freshly manicured hand.

He gave her a small smile and shook it carefully.

"Hello, Ms. Cassie."

"And I don't believe I've seen you around here before."

Oh boy. She was going to give him a hundred different questions. Funny, I still had an endless supply myself.

"No, mam. I stay over at Bevard's Resort."

"Oh, Bevard's."

They were the competing resort that sat a few miles down the lake.

She smiled and shook her head in agreement.

"So, what brings you HERE than?"

He turned towards me.

"Well, Brooke invited me."

She didn't miss a beat.

"Well, that was quite nice of you dear. But you've never once told us about this charming creature."

You have no idea.

She smiled hugely revealing her oversized dentures. I swore they looked two sizes too big for her mouth. She took another sip of her Gin while staring at Aaron.

"Well, I just only met him myself, Cassie."

"Well, how remarkable. I'm so glad you saw to it to come here and eat with us at one of Barb's parties. They are legendary here, and a good amount of fun too."

"Yes, they are nice people."

I couldn't wait to ask Aaron what she was thinking. By the twinkle in his eye, I could see probably a lot. Cassie was staring at his eyes too.

"Why dear, that is just so unusual."

Aaron looked up and wiped his face with a napkin. I could tell he was doing his best to blend in, and he was, but it was almost like having a famous movie star sitting next to you at the table. There would be no blending in. I could feel Cassie drumming up something to say, but the words weren't coming. She just sat and stared.

"Mam?"

"Oh, I'm sorry, where on earth are my manners? You'll have to forgive me; I don't think I've ever seen eyes that shade before. They are downright remarkable."

Of course, Ethel was following suit and staring now, too.

"Ethel, have you ever seen eyes like that?"

"No, I don't believe I have."

No matter what it was, if Cassie said it, Ethel always agreed with it. If Cassie said that clouds were purple, you better believe that Ethel would be chiming in about it too. It was just how it worked.

"Well, your grey eyes are a novelty. Do you get them from your mother or your father?"

I almost choked on my sandwich. Cassie was going all gangbusters.

"Well, thank you, but I do believe I got my eyes from my mother."

"Well, of course, you have dear. She must be very beautiful."

He smiled then, and for the first time, he looked genuinely touched by the sentiment.

"Why, thank you, Miss Cassie. Well, excuse me, but I think I need to get some more corn on the cob."

"See, you've done it now. You've embarrassed him Cassie, my goodness you are gonna run him out of the county."

I had to agree with Ethel.

"I think Aaron can handle a compliment. Men that pretty are used to being fussed over. I just call it as I see it, and that's one good-looking young man right there."

I smiled, Cassie always had a way of being right. I watched as Aaron picked at some more food from the other table. I knew he was reading their minds. I couldn't wait to find out. I couldn't help but think that maybe he was enjoying all this a little too much. They wouldn't find him all that attractive if his eyes started glowing all of a sudden. Ethel would have peed her pants. I was still nervous having Aaron interact with everyone. What if he had made some off comment, or suddenly acted strange?

But Aaron had perfect manners. And he never let on that he was different in the way that I knew him to be.

Mom sat down next to us. It was rare to see her sitting down and relaxing. Usually, she was always busy making sure everyone else had their plates full or drinks in hand. It was nice to see her sit down and chill for a few minutes.

"Well, is everyone doing ok here?"

Cassie moved over to the picnic table and patted the seat with her hand.

"We are fine Barb, you've more than outdone yourself. Why don't you sit and enjoy some dinner with us?"

"These corn on the cobs is just interesting on the grill Barb. The grill marks on it just make it so yummy."

"Well, I'm so glad you like it, Ethel."

Aaron gave me a little smile. I was going to have a field day with him as soon as I could get him alone. Reading minds. What a cool ability to have.

"Sometimes it is," he whispered in my ear.

I mouthed the words, 'Knock it off.'

He mouthed back...

"Ok, I'll turn it off, but that means I can't hear any of you and this is just too much fun."

I squinted my eyes at him. This was borderline ridiculous.

"Did I ever tell you the time I saw a UFO?" My mom blurted out.

"Oh, are we doing ghost stories? Well, all righty I just love that kind of story," Ethel said.

I looked over at Mom. I don't think I ever recalled her saying that she saw a UFO.

You did Mom?" I was very interested.

So was Aaron. He had stopped eating entirely, and his full attention was on mom.

Patti watched her intently. She was surprised as well.

"Well, yes I did. And by the way, you never asked."

That was true, but I always thought mom to be very analytical. She didn't seem to be the type to believe that kind of stuff, much less SEE one.

I couldn't believe it.

Cassie took the last sip from her gin and tonic.

"Where?" she asked.

"A few miles down the road."

"Oh, my. That close?" Ethel asked.

Ethel seemed as excited as a four-year-old getting candy.

"Well, let's start from the beginning. Your daddy was overseas in Vietnam…and it was a sweltering night. It had been a hot summer, and our house had no air conditioning. All I wanted to do was get out of that house.

Oh, we were young then, I was just barely in my twenties. Sometimes to pass away the evening, I would drive around the country roads to watch the deer graze the cornfields. I would find a spot I liked, then park alongside the road. Then I would just read.

Reading was a favorite pastime of mine. And I always brought my cat Penny with me. She was such a loyal, lap cat.

That evening was nothing out of the ordinary, really. I had made an early dinner, and then watched a little television. There wasn't really anything good on. So, after I finished the dishes, I thought I would go for a little drive. I did that a lot that summer. Sometimes, it could get really lonely without your dad, and that was a good way to pass the time."

I nodded my head.

"I usually liked parking by the farm fields, it was peaceful out there. You know the one on Highway D that goes on for miles and miles?"

"I like that little stretch of road." Cassie said.

"It was quiet that night. Usually you could hear wild life of some sort, but not that night. Anyway, after parking my car, I turned on my flashlight, and started reading. After about an hour, I was ready to leave. I remember thinking that it was strange that I hadn't seen even one deer. Usually they were always there, and in multiples. That was when I saw something coming down the road. At first, I thought it was a car with their headlights on full blast.

I just waved it on by, annoyed by how bright it was. Meanwhile, Penny was beside herself. She was digging her claws into the seats, meowing like crazy. This scared me the most, she had never acted that way before."

Ethel looked over at Cassie with wide eyes. They both hung onto her every word.

"Ok, what happened next Mom?" I asked.

"Well, I definitely felt like something was up. As I looked out my window, the whole cornfield looked lit up like a Christmas tree. Except this was way more than just some pretty, twinkling lights. There was this silver machine looking thing hovering over the fields about 100 yards away. It was massive, and egg-shaped to tell you the truth…..and looked to be steel-like. It was hanging high above the field like it was looking for something. I felt like I was the only person around for miles, and I didn't hear anything. Everything was quiet, except for Penny."

This was an all too familiar story. I looked over at Aaron. He was hanging on her every word.

"How long ago was this, may I ask?" Aaron said softly.

"Well, it's been close to 25 years now."

Aaron nodded.

"Sorry, continue please, don't let me stop you."

"Well, let's see, I wanted to get the hell out of there. But I tried turning the key, and just like a dumb horror movie, it wouldn't start back up."

"Oh heck, that always happens," Cassie said.

"Ain't that the truth," Ethel said.

"I kept trying and trying. It just wouldn't turn over. I was so scared I just knew that the car wasn't going to start again. And while I was trying to get away, this, machine had landed right in the middle of the field. I just couldn't believe it. It didn't make sense. But yet, there it was, plain as day, right in front of me. Then this weird, greenish colored light came out, and you could see even farther away. It lit up the farmland for miles. I knew it would only be a matter of time before they spotted my car."

Mom stopped and took a long sip of water. I could tell her story was making her scared all over again.

"Oh honey, I can't stand it. What happened next?"

Cassie tipped back the rest of her drink and was crunching forever on a piece of ice. She poured herself another.

"Well, it finally started. I slammed it into reverse, almost getting stuck in it. Poor Penny was underneath my feet meowing like crazy. She tucked herself under there and wouldn't move. I didn't even look out at the field anymore. I was too scared. I wasn't about to become one of their little lab experiments."

"Oh Lordy," Ethel gasped. She looked like she was about to faint.

"You ok, darling?"

"Yes mam, yes mam I am. Just give me a few minutes."

"This sort of thing just unnerves me a little bit. Well ok then, continue on doll."

We all had mom's attention.

"I just couldn't believe it. I could not believe what I was seeing. Especially that green light, it was so weird."

My mom stopped then to collect herself.

"Oh honey, I can't stand it. What happened next?" Cassie said.

"Well, I raced back home, and you know what? The whole time I was thinking that no one was ever going to believe me. When I got home, I called my mother-in-law. I explained what I saw. We even drove back to the field together. But nothing, and it was inky black out. Whatever it was, it was long gone. But she did believe me and convinced me to call the authorities. And I did, and surprisingly, they said I wasn't the only one who saw something that night. There were several other reports made and phone calls that evening about suspicious looking things in the sky. So that made me feel a little better, but not much."

"That must have scared the wits out of you," Ethel said.

"The whole experience was just strange, but I haven't seen anything like that since."

I looked over at Patti. Her eyes were as big as cue balls, and her mouth looked like it could drop down to the floor. I felt the same.

"Do you think it was from outer space? It wasn't a helicopter or anything?" Cassie asked.

"Christ, I hate that people think that I could have mistaken it for a helicopter. I know what they look like, and this clearly was not that."

"Well, that's a pretty good story. Anyone else got a scary tale to tell?" Ethel said.

Cassie looked up from her glass and stared out at the lake. She was unusually quiet.

"Well, I've got a doozy of a story."

"Cassie, you got a scary one too?" Patti asked.

I watched as Aaron sat there with pursed lips. If he knew something, he sure wasn't letting on that he did. I couldn't wait to talk to him alone. I wondered what he had heard, and whose mind he was reading now. To be honest, I didn't want him to know what Mom was thinking. That would just be plain wrong. Well, the whole thing kind of was wrong, but right now it seemed to be the only way to get answers. And if something they knew were a piece of the puzzle, I undoubtedly welcomed it.

Cassie always had a good laugh, and the theme usually revolved around her love life, pre-Lyles.

"Well, you know that I don't believe in ghosts and all that sort of bologna nonsense. But I did have a peculiar visitor one evening, a long, long time ago."

"Really Cassie?"

That got my attention, and Aaron's.

"Well, Lyle doesn't know much about this. He had been on a fishing trip that night. And please y'all don't tell him, it will just make him angry. You know he doesn't believe in any of it. I tried telling him, but he thinks it's all a lot of hogwash. He thinks I got myself too drunk and made up a story. Wait a minute, I need a fresh gin and tonic for this."

It was dark now. It had been for the past half hour. Mom had brought over a bowl of popcorn, and a bag of pretzels for us gathered at the picnic table. Cassie excused herself briefly to get a fresh drink.

"Bring me one too, will ya, hon?" asked Ethel.

"Sure, ole gal. But for you, I better bring the whole bottle of Vodka and maybe some Jack and Coke."

"You don't have to bring that," Mom said. "I've got plenty over here."

"Well, let's bring all of it out then for Christ sake."

As Cassie gingerly took the short walk to her cabin, she peeked my interest.

"Do you know what she's gonna say?"

"Oh, you better wait and let Cassie tell it. She would do it better justice."

A few long minutes later Cassie returned with a large bottle of Vodka and Rum in her hand. Mom had grabbed a fresh bag of ice in the freezer which she went inside to get, along with Coke and a couple of fresh glasses.

"Well, this makes me feel funny telling this. I mean, it's been ages." Cassie could pretend that she was embarrassed, but I knew her too well. She looked like she was right in her element, in fact.

"Oh no, this isn't *THAT* story is it?" Ethel asked.

"What are you talking about? I have lots of stories. And yes, I think at one time I told you this story when I was tipsy."

A ripple of laughter went through us. Cassie being tipsy wasn't a new phenomenon. It almost seemed like a requirement at every gathering. Her voice turned solemn.

"Well, this happened way back when. It was summer, and it happened right here at my house. Right here by your resort, Barb. He was actually at my doorstep."

"He? Who was at your door?" Mom asked suddenly.

"Well, let's back up a bit. Lyle and I had just bought the place, we had been living in it close to a month."

Mom nodded and followed her every word. We all did.

"Earlier that day I just remember it being so ungodly hot for living this far up north. Ya know, just sick, not wanting to step outside kind of hot."

"I remember that because it didn't get so hot back then. Not like it does now. For it to be that hot would be quite unusual."

"You know, I hate air conditioning, it's not natural," Ethel blurted out.

"Do you want me telling the story or not love?"

"Sorry, sshhhhhh," Ethel answered.

"Ok then. Well, as I said, it was a hot day, and the sky was stormy and angry for much of the afternoon. No rain though, it seemed like it wanted to rain, but couldn't decide if it should. Lyle of course, he was just his ole boring self. Getting ready for one of his fishing trips, and I didn't feel like joining him. Not on that day anyway. That night I was hard at work at a crossword puzzle, because the TV wasn't working right, no reception at all. That was another thing. Lights kept coming off and on earlier that evening. And I usually always have my hair dryer plugged in, that damn thing kept turning on by itself in the bathroom. I turned that thing off three times. I didn't understand that one. Couldn't be explained, and that gave me the absolute willies, finally had to unplug the darn thing. Then next was the fridge, it had turned off, lost power. Nothing seemed to work. But then it would come back on, and then it wouldn't.

I tried getting a hold of Lyle, but he was already somewhere down at the lake, fishing in one of his fishing holes. And I just didn't know what to make of it, I thought I was going crazy. And I hate it when my TV doesn't work, remember, we didn't have cable back then. All we had was plain old rabbit ears, and all you could get was three different channels. Well, felt like all my appliances were ganging up on me. That's when I thought I would stroll on over to your house Barb to see if you had the same things happening."

"I remember that night!" Mom said.

"We had the same sort of thing going on. And you stayed over for a while."

"Yes, we played cards. But then it was getting late, and I wanted to head on back, even though it was just a fifty-foot walk. Now, I always leave my door open, because why the hell not? I just have a screen door is all, and no one messes with anyone else, so I didn't think twice about keeping it unlocked. And everything was just the same when I walked in. Except, my little Yorkie at the time, Buttons was barking and caring on like you wouldn't believe.

"Ever since I stepped back to the cabin, it was almost as if he was allergic to me or something. Running around in circles, looking out at the lake, pressing his little nose against the screen door. It gave me the creeps. He was hysterical. Something wasn't sitting right with him. And I could tell! I felt it too. Someone was there *or had been there.*

"Now I can't tolerate being scared in my own home. But that night, I was. But I really couldn't figure out why, just an innate sense that I was not alone, and I was being watched."

Oh, how I knew the feeling.

"Now, this feeling stuck with me and wouldn't leave. Since I was already up, I figured I would make myself a pot of tea. Just to help ease my mind about things. And I knew Lyle kept a shotgun in our back bedroom, so I went and got the thing out. I didn't know if it was loaded or nothing, but I felt better with it in my hands. It was heavy, and I was shaking.

So, I sat down and watched that tea kettle at the stove. I felt the need to have it at arm's length, I quickly checked, and it was already loaded, thank Christ. And don't you know, just as soon as I set it down, I heard the faintest tap at the door. Like three little light knocks in a row. I couldn't imagine who would be coming by at that hour. But it was probably the thing I was waiting for."

Cassie took a little breath and another sip of her drink. It shook in her hands.

"Who was it? Who was at the door Cassie?" asked Ethel.

Ethel reminded me of a young child asking for another cookie.

"Well, that's an interesting question."

"Why?" We all asked in unison.

"Well, what I saw looked like someone who was lost. But believe me, it was a big put on, a formality if you will. I remember him being tall, like a long, string bean. And his face looked like he had put on a coat of pancake foundation, in the ghastliest shade of white you can imagine."

Leave it to Cassie to get technical with her colors.

"He was dressed all tidy in a black suit, with his hair jet black to match. I couldn't see his eyes because he was wearing sunglasses. It gave me the willies."

"Oh, is this the man in black story?"

"Oh Ethel, now hush."

"Now, I didn't want this whatever-it-was setting foot inside my place. The situation wasn't right. *He wasn't right.* He might have been funny looking, but not ha-ha funny. His mannerisms, were not human, not of a regular person."

I had chilly goosebumps. I looked over at Aaron. His eyes hadn't left hers since she started. I wondered so much what he was thinking. But he had no expression.

"Have you ever seen Texas Chainsaw Massacre? He looked like chainsaws creepy sidekick. Same pasty look to his face."

"I asked him what he wanted. He said he wanted to ask me a few questions, and I told him it was too late for questions because it was."

"Did he look like the devil?" Karen asked.

"No, but something about him didn't seem to be of this earth. That I was sure of, he smelled of it. And then he just helped himself in, and slowly took off his sunglasses, revealing the iciest blue eyes that I had ever seen in my darn life. Like two jagged pieces of ice glaring right into me.

Felt like he was baring down deep into my soul, and without my permission, I may add.

He got me so rattled I barely could remember my own name. He could have busted right through my wimpy screen if he wanted to, but instead, he chose to knock, so I figured I'd just listen to his questions, I got the feeling he was going to ask me whether I wanted him to or not."

"Oh, crap!" Mom said. She looked very nervous.

"I offered him a drink, I don't know why, but it just seemed like the thing to do. He said no, he wouldn't be staying long enough for a drink. But when he walked in like that, he seemed so curious about everything that I had in there, and at the most mundane things too.

"YOU LET HIM IN THE HOUSE???" Ethel said.

"He let himself in Ethel! What was I to do? Like a screen door was gonna keep him away. I just pretended that I always received visitors at two in the morning."

I turned and looked over at Aaron. He was engrossed in her story, but he gave me a little reassuring squeeze on my hand.

"I didn't want to turn my back on this stranger. And I think he did read my mind because he suddenly said, 'Not to worry mam, not to worry. There are no worries here.'

"Do you think he was a man?"

"Course he had man-like features, but nothing about that thing was right or human. The milky shade of his skin looked like it hadn't seen a ray of sunshine in his entire life. Oh, and that cologne of his, the notes on that were something else. Very woodsy and floral, kind of like pine needles, but sharper. And he seemed very interested in Buttons. Bless Buttons little heart, that dog wasn't having anything to do with him. He crawled under that kitchen table and planted himself right against the heating register as soon as he heard that knock on the door. He rolled up into a little ball, like if he played dead maybe milk face would go away.

He said he was from the FBI and wanted to know if I had seen anything suspicious that day because there had been a murder.

"A murder, in NEELSVILLE?" said Ethel.

"I know, crazy!" Cassie said. "Well, I told him I didn't know anything about a murder."

"What did he do next?" Karen asked.

"He thought it was funny. He laughed his rail-thin butt off. I mean, I don't know how talking about murder could be so darned funny. I did ask him why he was still wearing sunglasses when it was nighttime. And do you know what he said? It was because his eyes were light sensitive. Sounds like a standard pat-ass answer if you ask me. So anyway, he starts snooping around in my cupboards, opening up drawers, staring at my utensils. He was so intrigued by my kitchen table, he knelt down to look underneath. Like I had a body hidden there or something. And you should have seen Buttons, he almost bit him. He was growling something fierce. Well, milk face got the hint because he got right back up.

I have to say, he was polite, for all outside purposes, despite every bone in my body telling me he was everything but. He never

had an edge to his voice, and he seemed very controlled in his questioning. In fact, to this day I can't believe I even let him in the door."

"Oh Cassie, did he rape you?" Ethel asked puzzled.

"Christ, no Ethel, he didn't rape me."

Cassie took another long sip.

"He did ask if he could have a glass of water. I said no problem, and when I went over to get him one, he gazed at the glass like
he's never seen one before. I noticed then his thin gold wedding
band on his finger. I couldn't begin to think how that thing could
be married. Anyway, he finished it in one long gulp, and that was
a tall glass mind you. It was just all so bizarre."

"I wonder if this was around the time I saw that UFO?"
Mom asked.

"It may have been."

"What else did he ask you?" I asked

"Well, he jotted a few things down on this small notepad he
took from his pocket. He asked me where I was from, if I always
lived here, and how many brothers and sisters that I have…if I had
any children."

Aaron looked visibly upset. It seems like this whole story
pained him.

"Did you ask him what these questions had to do with
a murder?"

"Well yeah, but he sort of just went on with his speech, damn
if I could recall it. It was almost like I was drugged or something."

Cassie made her voice to a whisper to emphasize her point,
*"Let me tell y'all. I know everything about what's going on in this
town, and there was no strange occurrence like a murder. I even*

asked Margie down at the bar if anybody had come into her place asking funny questions. She said no. It's just all really disturbing."

"How did you finally get him out of there?" Mom asked.

"Well, I felt that I answered enough of his questions and it was time for him to be leaving or I would be calling the police, ASAP. He said there would be no need for that, and he put his tiny shaded glasses back on and turned around robotic like and walked out the door. And poof, he vanished. Gone. He was fast, I'll give him that. No car, no tracks, no nothing. The only thing he left was the smell of pine needle cologne.

And the way he dressed made me think he would have a car. Why would someone like that come to my door asking about a murder? And at that hour??"

Cassie was finished with her story. And her drink, too. She looked drained from both.

"What do you make of it Cassie?" Mom asked.

Ethel spoke up.

"Alien. She thinks he was an alien."

Mom started picking up some of the other cocktail glasses, most of which were empty. I could see her hands were shaky, too.

"You know, come to think of it, I remember that hot day because it was around the same time that I saw that UFO. It must have been sometime in July."

"Well, I would have to agree with ya. I know, because Lyle always takes his fishing trips in July. Every year for the last twenty of them, that I know of."

"Have you ever seen him again, Cassie?" Karen asked.

"No. That was it, thank Christ."

Margie had been listening the whole time while looking like she saw a ghost.

"Someone like that might have visited my bar."

We all turned around.

"Yeah, I remember him. He was a tall, kinda slippery looking fellow. He was creepy, reminded me of a dark, twisted twig off a tree. I bet he was the same person you saw Cassie."

"Well good golly. At least this confirms my sanity. Cause honestly, I had to question it myself sometimes."

"I remember when he walked in, he made me nervous, too. I was the only one tending bar. And he ordered the strangest drink, a Rob Roy. I remember my customers by the drink they order, and I never forget a drink. I don't really care much for making those fancy types. About the fanciest I get is a screwdriver."

That got a few chuckles from the group.

"I said I don't make drinks like that, but he could have a beer if he wanted."

"So, what did you do?"

"I gave him a beer."

"Did he have teeth, Marjorie?" Cassie asked.

"I don't remember. I didn't like looking at him for too long."

"Oh, I remember that! I didn't like making eye contact either. Gave me the creeps," Cassie said.

"Man, I haven't thought about that in a long time. Lots of different types come in now and again, but I never forgot him."

The evening was winding down, and we were all ready to be done with stories and get some sleep.

"It goes to show you that some things in this world just cannot be explained by science, common sense, or anything. No matter how illogical it may seem. There are just some strange things that happen in life, and you just have to roll with it. Gain insight from experience. And oh Christ, just take it from there."

"Well, thank you for the story, Cassie."

"Yes, thanks, Cassie. Well, maybe we should keep our eyes out for pencil thin men dressed in black," Mom said.

There was laughter, but it was the nervous kind.

"Not a bad idea," Margie said. "I will keep my eyes open at the bar."

I could tell Aaron needed to talk to me alone. And I wanted to talk to him alone. I had wanted to do that all night. Was this what he was warning me about? Were these the distractors?

When it was comfortable for us to leave the group, we found a small private area together. But we didn't have much time. I know mom was going to tell me any minute it was time for bed. It was already late.

"This is exactly what I was afraid of."

Aaron looked upset.

"What they saw, Aaron is that what you were warning me about?"

He looked over at me, and I could detect pity. He only nodded.

"I think so. You guys are in more danger than I realized. They've been scanning this area, and for a long time."

"What does that mean?"

"They want this place for something. There's probably something here that they need."

"You mean, you're not saying they are going to turn us into them, are you?"

"I have to do some intensive investigating. But this is very dangerous, for all of you, I'm afraid."

I panicked. Would they turn my family and friends into that red-eyed thing I encountered days before? The thought made me sick to my stomach.

"Listen, distractors can only turn the weak minded, but believe me, they have their ways. They are tricky, *very tricky*. In fact, considering what I just heard, I wouldn't be surprised if someone you already know is one."

What?

I could not believe what I was hearing.

"You don't mean anybody close to me, do you?"

"Nobody I sat with at the party is, at least not yet. I would have known. I am an ally of yours. They know that. And they are going to want to get rid of me, believe me. But knowing they were here twenty years ago is not a comforting thought. Time means nothing to them.

Twenty years can be ten minutes for them. They are innate creatures, can adapt to any environment, and they are brilliant. I'm going to have to go back, just for a few days, Brooke. And I can't do this alone. I need to bring some help with me, some backup."

"Are they nice?"

It was the only question I could come up with, and I knew it sounded dumb. But I was scared, and I sure wanted them to be pleasant.

"It's my brother and a few others. And I'm sure he'll want to know what's going on here as well."

"I want to come with you."

"Listen, they are not coming for a while. I would know, I can sense when they are here. So, you guys are safe until then. Where I'm going, you don't want to come. You can't adapt to it. I will be back, I promise."

I was crying. This was all way too much.

"But what if you don't come back?"

"I'll come back to you, I promise."

His grey eyes were blazing. He was mesmerizingly handsome, and I could have looked at him all day.

He was reading my mind again.

"I can't be distracted, ok? Though you are a lovely distraction, I need to keep my wits about me. Do you understand?"

He put his hand softly on my cheek. A simple, loving gesture, which I loved. I turned my face into his hand and kissed it. Quickly his lips found mine, and he was gentle at first, but before I knew it, I felt a strong hand against the back of my head. He was strong in his kiss, and he wanted control, that was for sure. And I was happy to be lost in it. I felt like I was floating way up in a cloud. He finished kissing me on the side of my neck. And as his face left mine, my neck and lips felt the tingling after effects. And of course, wanting more.

"I promise you, Brooke. Give me a week or two. I will see you as soon as I get back. I will tell you everything that you want or need to know. But this is important, you must not let on what you know, Brooke. Promise me. TELL NO ONE. It seems talking of them attracts them as well. Any suspicion, anything not ordinary for humans to discuss. Promise me!"

He ran his hand through his coppery hair.

"Ok, look."

He showed me the back of his neck.

"I'm gonna give you a quick, down and dirty lesson. A distractor has pretty distinct markings. This isn't true of all, but some have a set of numbers on the back of their neck."

"What?"

"Their eyes will be different as well. That's an obvious one though, like the red-eyed bastard you encountered."

"But some of them will blend in perfectly. It will be harder to detect. And they have a certain smell about them. But I wouldn't go by that-they can change that daily. Now if you think you see one, stop talking to them immediately. Do you understand? Go straight home. But don't make it too obvious if you know what I mean. I know I'm not making much sense right now."

"This is scaring me, Aaron."

"I know, but odds are, they are not around here. Not for now at least. But they want to be, that's obvious. They probably think this is the perfect place because it's so secluded and out of the way."

My heart was pounding in my chest. What was I going to do? Knowing my luck, some of them were already here.

"Listen, they think things through very thoroughly. They don't want to make themselves known unless their life is in danger. But promise, just be careful, ok? I'll be back before you know it, and I will bring reinforcements."

"Ok, I promise. But what if you don't come back?"

That was my very worst fear.

"I will."

Right then I thought about, grandma. I thought about how she told me she would be back.

"And, I'm going to give you something, this should give you a little edge on things."

"What?"

"Believe me, you'll know it when you get it. That's all I am allowed to say."

There seemed to be so many rules in his world. But I went along with it.

Aaron brought both his hands to either side of my cheeks and stared at me for a few long moments. His eyes were mesmerizing. Before I knew it, whatever he was doing, he was done. It felt like my head was buzzing.

"What did you do to me?"

"You'll be ok, I promise."

And with that, he was gone in a flash.

I watched with sad eyes as he left. My boyfriend, the alien, was somewhere deep in the woods, finding a way back to his home.

And I was standing in a daze, feeling like my head was on fire. I didn't like how strongly attached I already was to him. It made me feel more vulnerable than I wanted to.

But the heart wants what it wants. There was no stopping it, and it couldn't be helped.

THE GIFT

*E*verywhere I looked now I was looking for signs of a distractor. It's the first thing I thought of when I awoke in the morning. It was what I thought of when I was silently eating my cereal. It was what I half expected to see whenever I looked out my window.

Thank God we were still on summer break.

Every morning I would do a running check with my family: Mom, Dad, and Patti. When I was satisfied that they hadn't turned into a monster overnight; I would move on to people that I knew or saw, at the resort or in town. Aaron said to look for odd things that didn't seem to match.

I did this as I went about my day. I didn't want to be paranoid, but it was necessary. I couldn't help but be frightened out of my mind one minute, then when nothing seemed out of the ordinary, I could finally calm down enough to sit. But that usually wasn't for very long. I found it helped to keep my hands busy. Knitting worked, but my hands shook like I was pumped up with caffeine. My nerves were working me over, and I longed for an easy chore to take my mind off it. Until then, I had no choice but to just live with it.

Aaron said they wouldn't touch my family now. But I kept asking how he could be so sure? He told me that since he has been around the area and at the resort, that my family and I were safe. They didn't like going anywhere near Aaron or his 'type.' And they can sense this and know that he's dangerous and would stay away. He kept reassuring me, but I had my doubts.

Time means something different to them than it does to us. And they have lots and lots of both.

I wanted to tell my family, especially Patti. I shuddered to think of what would happen if she would come in contact with someone who was infected. Or any other innocent person? We would have to start fighting them. Aaron was going to have to hurry up and let me in on how to fight them. Because I wanted to know.

He said there might be people I already know that have already turned into distractors.

I thought immediately of June. That would have made perfect sense! And would also explain her odd behavior. I was obsessed now with wondering who possibly could be one. And who I might have come in contact over the years that might have been. It rattled me to the core.

I grabbed a lemonade and walked up to the pool. The can was so cold, I wanted to set it down. The humidity was oppressive in the air. Mom was tending to resort things, Dad was at work. Patti was probably off reading a book somewhere. It was a typical, lazy, summer day.

And I was busy combing through everyone in my line of sight to make sure they weren't a monster.

If they only knew the things that I knew.

Yeah, then I'd be sent away with all the other crazies at Woods View.

People were happily going about their day, and I was on pins and needles trying to keep the boogeyman at bay.

The same phrase kept echoing over and over in my head.

Were these things going to take over everything? And when? And how were they going to do it? When was it going to start in our town?

Who knew a simple trip to the grocery store could be a mind-altering experience. I guess profound things can happen right smack in the middle of a rather uneventful day. My life changed for a second time while in the parking lot of Nielson's grocery store. It was a subtle thing at first when I noticed it while walking in the parking lot. It was more of a feeling than hearing the actual words.

And it was then that I thought I was going cuckoo. You'd think that would have happened back when I first saw Aaron, or when the tree came to life, or seeing that red-eyed nightmare. Take your pick.

It was someone's voice, and it sure wasn't mine. There's really not a great way to explain what it feels like to hear another voice echo through your head, and knowing it's not your own.

It's frightening. You find yourself looking around, wondering if anyone else can hear them. Accept everyone else is minding their own business, and could care less. Nope, I'm the only crazy person here. Great.

There are special places for people like that. This wouldn't be an easy subject to approach to anyone, unless of course you wanted some street cred with the other crazies at the mental hospital. Perhaps they wouldn't judge, but maybe think that you were such a special breed of crazy that they would leave you alone.

No, this was nothing like that. But as I was walking outside taking a simple visit to our towns' grocery store, I heard a faint voice in my head. And the more I tried to ignore it, it only got louder, like it was daring me to respond.

Not fair...stupid...screwed up my life...parents would never understand....

These idle words ran through my mind in quick, repeated patterns, over and over. Trying to focus in on it was like trying to tune into a radio station. I tried to push back my own thoughts and thinking so I could concentrate on these outside phrases. This wasn't easy to do, ignoring your thoughts felt unnatural and strange, like opening your eyes under water. But just the same, I seemed I had an apparent ability to decipher between the two.

A young teenage girl rushed past me. She wasn't having the best day by the looks of it. She walked quickly toward the store's front doors like her life depended on it. It didn't take long to figure out that this was the girl I was hearing.

No. This can't happen to me.

I focused on her, which made her thoughts come in more clearly.

I don't want to be pregnant. Why didn't we just use something?? I cannot take care of a baby. I can barely take care of myself. I want lip gloss. I don't want to spend money on a frickin' pregnancy test. And God, diapers are so expensive...

The more I heard, the more I wanted to keep listening. I was feeling pangs of guilt about this, but I shoved that aside. I picked up my pace so I could get closer, without being too conspicuous. She made her way to the health and beauty aisle towards the pregnancy tests section. I watched as she eyed all the different brands, settling on one of the cheaper brands, and putting it in her basket. Right then her thoughts came to me crystal clear. If the test came out positive, she was going to get rid of it.

And there I stood a couple of feet away thinking, '*HOLY#&$ I can hear every thought that you are thinking!!!!*'

I felt like I swallowed a box of dynamite. I was so terrified I wanted to jump out of my skin. As she walked past me toward the next aisle, her thoughts became more muted, until I finally couldn't hear them anymore. Guess she was out of my range.

I stood there in a stupor. What had just happened? And why was I able to hear her?

I nervously looked over towards the direction of my mom. She was in the bakery aisle eyeing some donuts. She usually liked having one with her coffee in the morning.

Did I really want to know? Miserably I stood there waiting to hear any other noise that might be my mother. Bracing myself for something I didn't want to experience. To my surprise, I couldn't get any read from her.

THANK GOD.

I looked over toward Patti. No thoughts were coming through from her either. Maybe it didn't work on relatives. I breathed a huge sigh of relief. I felt like I sidestepped a land mine. Good. I didn't much care to hear what my family was thinking anyway.

I nervously looked around the store. I wondered…is this ability with just one person or many? And why her? I needed to find out. I tried walking casually over towards the meat aisle. I could feel sharp jabs at my temple, like someone was trying to get my attention. It felt like one doozy of a headache. Mom was looking at hamburger, and the guy behind her looked like he was two steps away from hot steam tooting out of his ears.

And I could hear exactly what he was thinking.

He was about to tell her to get &*$ out of his way, except in a flash he did a complete turnaround since when he saw her face, he thought her somewhat attractive. Ok, this was taking strange turns. I could feel my palms getting sweaty. I felt like blinders had been taken off that I didn't even realize I had.

More jabs at my temples again, like an electrical current was running through my head. Like some long dormant ability had been awakened.

The only thoughts swirling about in my head now were my own. Whatever force that gave me this ability had come and gone, and very quickly; it had left.

I took a deep breath, in and out. My first thoughts were of relief. I walked around to the candy aisle and pretended to ogle over a bag of gobstoppers.

There was a little girl who had been sitting on the floor whom I guessed to be about three next to me, and a teenager on my other side. From the look on his hard face, he was clearly bothered by something. His face was full of acne, one on top of the other. For some reason, I felt compelled to read his thoughts. I tried willing my new ability back, but it didn't work. All I could hear was the zombie-inducing music filtering from the store speaker.

Ok, this was going to take a lot more than twitching my nose and snapping my fingers, but how? I *wanted* to know what people were thinking. Especially this boy who looked like he wanted to kill every living, breathing soul that was walking into the store.

Maybe if I thought hard enough, it would come back. I tried reaching out with my mind and blocking out any outside interferences.

At first, there was nothing, just the nervousness of my own thoughts. And then, there it was...that jab at my temple again.

I swear I could hear my own heartbeat. And it was getting louder by the second...and then.

What dicks! One of these days they will get what is coming to them.

I jumped at the start of his voice. It was the boy, of course, he looked over at me for a second, but continued eyeing what was down the aisle. It would appear that the closer I was, the more clear the thoughts became. And his were dark and heavy.

He was a swirling mixture of anger and it was uncomfortable to feel. I could tell that I wouldn't be able to read his mind much longer and not be affected by it. Very different from what I picked up from the girl. From her, it was more thoughts of loneliness, isolation, and fear. From him, I could feel rage, and a strong sense of righting a wrong.

He didn't have a very good day at school. He was tired of being bullied. I suppose this would have been an obvious guess by anyone just looking at him. But from me, I could *feel* it with him.

Someone had humiliated him deeply, and it was all he could think about. He kept replaying the events over and over in his head. Those few details were out of the realm of pulling apart, but it was evident he was upset, and he was determined to get them all back. I'm assuming he meant his classmates.

It made me nervous standing this close while peering into his thoughts. I knew I was overstepping my boundaries here. I half expected at any minute he would start yelling at me for finding out, but he didn't. He just turned down the next aisle, and I was glad for it. In the small moments that his angry thoughts had mingled with mine, I could feel his anger trying to seep its way in. I was getting mad to, even thou they were not my thoughts.

This all took an immediate toll, and I was left feeling like I hadn't had water in days. I realized that if I was going to do this, I needed to learn how to separate my thoughts from the others that I could read.

With him down the next aisle, I noticed movement down at my feet. It was a little girl, who looked to be around three years old. There were no jabs at the temples. I smiled at her. Her mind felt light and whimsical, like warm rays of sunshine. A welcome relief from what I just experienced.

I could tell right away she was a perceptive little thing, most children were. But as her mom edged closer with her grocery cart, the girls' thoughts started reading fuzzy. They seemed to be getting blocked by something. I think her mom's thoughts were getting mixed in, and she was under the influence of something. Several different mind-altering drugs maybe, but I couldn't tell you what.

She was happy it was Friday. She was looking forward to being able to enjoy a drink by herself, in the privacy or her own home. She didn't like going out much, she didn't like crowds, and she loathed going to the grocery store.

It was the little things that gave her the most anxiety. She had managed to scrape enough together to buy the largest bottle of Jack Daniels she could find. And now it was resting sideways quite comfortably next to her purse in the cart. Just seeing the bottle had made her mouth water. She couldn't wait to get the rest of her boring groceries so she could make good friends with that bottle. She eyed a bag of Lays potato chips and put them in.

As she bent down to pick up the girl, I could smell cigarettes and stale bar. She looked older than she probably was. Her eyes were huge and glossy; you'd think she had been high for most of the week. I was fascinated. Her mind read all over the place, but it was hard to nail down a precise, concrete thought; her nerves and anxiety kept creeping in.

I wondered then if she had some sort of psychological problem like schizophrenia. Her hair was limp, and the color of rats, with the ends bleached out white or had been. She was probably quite a looker in high school, but that ship had clearly sailed. It wouldn't take a genius to figure out why.

Part of me knew I was unfair, listening in on her private thoughts. Part of me wanted to lift up that little girl up and take her away from her unfit mother. I suddenly wanted to know what everyone was thinking in the store. It was like I got a free pass to the coolest party ever, how could I throw out the invitation?

I saw a man up ahead, and he seemed nice enough. I strolled towards him, pretending to be fixated on the price of tombstone pizzas. It was chilly down that aisle, so I hurried on past. As I did, it was like someone turned up the volume on a TV. He had creepy eyes. I didn't really care to know what he was really thinking. Thankfully, Mom came walking up.

"There you are, what are you doing?"

Um, you really don't want to know.

"Nothing, I was about to look at some magazines."

"Ok, but I'm getting ready to go in a few minutes."

Off in the distance, I could see Guy walking over towards the deli. He looked like he was in a hurry.

Oh no. Did I want to know? Funny, to think of how many times I had wanted to know what he was thinking, here the opportunity was dangling like a carrot right in front of me. Wouldn't it be nice to know what he was thinking once and for all?

He noticed me and slowly came walking up. Well, it was go time, now or never. I tried to smile, be my usual self, whatever that was nowadays.

He had that trademark grin on his face. I couldn't help but smile.

"So, you do actually eat? I would have never thought it stretch."

"Yep. But only on special occasions."

I tried to be as witty as possible. The situation called for it. Either that or run like a bat out of hell out the store. But since I couldn't do either...

Before he could get another sentence out, I could detect his thoughts. Part of me really and honestly didn't want to know, but I listened. At first, his thoughts were like a whisper. They lacked strength, and ran in no-nonsense bursts.

This is strange. I don't feel right. Man, I'm tired. I could use a nap. Why am I so hungry? I just ate a ton for lunch....boy, it's nice to see her. Man, I could really use a nap today.

His mind was racing, and repeating, and it felt uneasy. He was bothered by something. And there was another thing, something unlike who I knew Guy to be.

He was scared.

Why was Guy so scared?

His uneasiness was out of tune with how I knew him to be. And because my mind registered something else from him, my face blushed because of it. You'd think I could start to control that.

He was wondering what it would be like to kiss me.

Right then and there, it was a fleeting moment, and if I wasn't so focused on listening in on him, I might not have caught it. But I did. I looked down and pretended to concentrate on the rather drab tile floor. I noticed the spackling was uneven and thick on one side...whoever did that job; they didn't take their time with it.

Oh crap, talking to him like this was going to be difficult, subconsciously or not.

"Whatcha buying?"

"Stocking up on the essentials, you know beer, crawlers. Going out to fish later."

"Oh, yeah."

This was one of these times that I was genuinely speechless. And it was almost a good thing that the older lady further down the aisle decided to walk past both of us when she did.

And unfortunately for me, I was just as floored to hear that she was just as turned on by Guy as I was.

How was it that I was encountering so many horny, old people in this store? I didn't know what that said about our town.

"What's up with you?"

I had to keep my wits about me.

And now he was wondering if I found him attractive. Oh crap, I should turn this off right now. I needed to get out of there quick before I gave it all away.

"Mom's probably wondering about me, I'll see you later."

"Ok."

When I got farther enough away, his thoughts had faded away to.

THANK GOD.

As I stood behind Mom at the checkout, I started hearing random, odd thoughts from the cashier. She wanted to be at Nielsen's like she wanted a hole in her head. Mom didn't seem to notice, she was busy writing in her checkbook.

The last thing I wanted to do right now was listen to the unconscious thoughts of Neilson's cashier. My temples were buzzing, and I wanted to leave. If I didn't get something to drink or eat shortly, I was probably going to need help off the floor.

The cashier was going to give someone named Eileen a tongue lashing once she saw her again. And that was me leaving out a few choice details.

She didn't bother with any sort of greeting as she started passing our food across the scanner.

Don't attract attention to yourself.

Ok, hearing all these thoughts I was starting to feel crowded. I needed a break. I stood there and closed my eyes for a moment, silently willing it away.

And as soon as I did, it left. Good. That was easy. I just need a little bit of a break. I couldn't imagine having this on all the time, my brain would combust.

As Patti, Mom, and I walked out the store I recognized one of the town winos in the parking lot. He was one of a few that hung around the two grocery stores and gas station that made up Neelsville. They hung around the taverns like bees to honey. Not being able to help myself, I stupidly turned on my gift again. I was learning pretty quickly that turning it off and on wasn't too bad.

But instead of hearing him (I guess he was too far away) I heard someone else.

That cashier was as dense as a two-brick fireplace.

It was one of my classmates. She saw me to, but didn't keep eye contact. She gave me a dismissive wave and walked to her car. She was in a hurry, and her mind was reading, *high as a kite*, but not from any drug.

This high was not chemically produced.

This was high in its purest of forms: adrenaline. My classmate just stole a handful of Cover Girl makeup from the beauty aisle. Her coat pockets were jammed packed full of it. She wasn't going to do it at first. But she really wanted that mascara, the lipstick and so on. So, at the last moment, she decided to buy a soda, to not seem too obvious. One pocket was jammed with makeup, while the other was full of change that she counted out for the soda.

No one had noticed. And to top it off, the clerk gave her a friendly smile and told her to have a nice day. She would now.

And I would have never thought her to be a thief. In school, she came across to me as Miss Goody two shoes. This revelation made me wonder about people.

I felt like I was on a mental tread mill. And I did not doubt that this new ability of mine involved Aaron.

Who has the power to do that?

I couldn't help but think that he must be some sort of God or something to be able to do that. Whatever he was, he had some explaining to do. I couldn't wait for him to get back in town. All I could think about was how Aaron and I could help save Neelsville, before it became overrun with distractors.

I decided that for now, I would definitely need a break. I was thankful for the quiet ride home. My mind was exhausted and tired. And I felt like I had so much to learn. I felt like I joined in on this supernatural party a bit too late.

THE LEFT-OVERS

*G*uy wasn't looking so good. Course he didn't look very well at the store either. But I really noticed it at the party last night, but it wasn't enough for me to mention it to Aaron. They had left early, either from a fight or whatever. And now it was too late to tell Aaron. Aaron was probably a million miles away from me. The thought made me momentarily sick.

I stared at the tinfoil that covered a large plate of food that I was walking over to Guy and Lisa's. Before my knuckle could knock on the screen door, Lisa's face appeared out of nowhere. I guess she saw me coming up. Seeing her made me jump, and I nervously smiled at her.

I was hoping that Guy would be the one to answer it, so my heart sank a little when I saw her. And without thinking about it, I turned on my new ability to read.

"Well, hello, Brooke."

Maybe something in my subconscious realized that it was in my best interest to read her mind. Or could it be fight or flight kicking in? Whatever the reason, I was glad for it. She was pleasant for all outside purposes. But as I tried mentally to pick her brain so to speak, I immediately felt hers close off, as if she shut the door to it right then and there. It felt like a mental vault slammed down. All this with a huge smile on her face. I sure hoped she couldn't tell I was doing this. But if she did, she sure wasn't letting on.

"Hi, Lisa. We had a bunch of food left over, Mom thought maybe you'd like some."

She eyed it curiously.

"Oh yes, thanks. We can nibble on that later."

Picturing Lisa nibbling on anything was a stretch. I don't think I've seen her eat anything period.

I'm sure my plate of food would soon be in the trash as soon as I left. That was ok with me. The woman gave me the creeps; she could do whatever she wanted as long as I wasn't around. I stood there wondering what to say next. It was too bad I couldn't get any read from her. It would have been nice to figure out what she thought of me once and for all.

Her demeanor towards me was always rather chilly, and today was no different. This morning she was still looking her smartly put together self. Her hair wound up in a tight little bun, not a strand out of place of course.

"Where's Guy?"

"Oh, he's in bed. I'm afraid he's not himself today."

My nerves picked up.

"Is he ok?"

"Oh yes, he's fine. But, I think he may have come down with something. He'll be up and around shortly I'm sure. You can peek in on him if you like."

I was surprised at the invite, but I took it.

"Thank you."

I anxiously followed her down the narrow hallway. Guy and sick? The two words just didn't mesh. Guy was never sick. I didn't even remember him ever having a cold. Granted I only saw him for a few weeks over the summer, but still, he wasn't someone that portrayed weakness in any form.

Lisa stopped short of the bedroom and stood in the doorway. I looked in and saw Guy's head, peeking out from under the covers, much like a child would be. The cast to his skin reminded me a little bit of that cake with grey icing, except his was a shade lighter.

It looked weird and out of place, and it didn't suit him. Usually he was always tan. I wanted Lisa to leave so I could talk to him alone. I didn't feel comfortable talking to him with her hovering around.

"Well, aren't you a sight."

"Stretch."

I was glad to hear Lisa's heels clicking her way back down the hall. I found it odd that she would be wearing heels in her cabin while on vacation. Too bad she just couldn't get on her broomstick and fly herself away.

I could hear faint trickles of Guy's thoughts enter my mind. They were feeble and weak, but I could still read them.

It was apparent right away that he was pre-occupied. Much like how he was at the store, except now those thoughts were more desperate. And in between his racing thoughts, I would get little hiccups, or just small spots of void, nothing. One moment he was thinking how bad he hated lying there, feeling helpless, and the next moment his thoughts were getting scrambled up with something else. And I couldn't detect this something else. He sensed my questioning.

"Just ate something that didn't agree with me."

Alright Guy, if that's the explanation you want to use, so be it. I wasn't buying it.

"That's what Lisa said. But I thought you had a cast iron stomach."

He attempted a small grin, but his eyes were anxious.

"You look terrible."

"Well, gee thanks, appreciate you, too."

"Sorry. Is there anything I can get for you?"

I sat on the edge of the bed and stared at the man who two days ago, was jumping in pools, had muscles for days, and looked fit as a gladiator. Today he looked like a deflated version of his former self.

"Do something for me, ok?"

"Of course, Guy. What is it?"

I bent down so I could better hear his words.

"You have to leave."

"What? Why"

I didn't understand.

"Not here, this place. There are things…. There are things here…I can't really explain it to you right now…"

I whispered as quietly as I could.

"I know. Be strong, ok? We're going to figure this thing out."

I held my breath. I hoped Lisa couldn't hear.

I whispered back.

"Don't say anything more."

While Guy was talking, Lisa just so happened to be standing in the doorway. Of course, she was. I hoped she didn't hear us.

She was wearing something over the top and summery. I could see that on the inside she was a clever wolf in sheep's clothing. I don't know if I knew this because of my gift, or maybe it was something I always knew. But right now, Guy was in grave danger, and it made me itchy having to talk with her in that room.

My first impulse was to get away, but I couldn't, not just yet. I could feel little welts forming on my back. Great, she was literally giving me hives.

I turned back to Guy, but he was already asleep.

The room was jarring and claustrophobic. Since he was asleep, there wasn't much for me to do. It was time for me to leave.

"Get some rest Guy, I'll check up on you later."

I hated to leave, but I didn't know what else I could do. I walked back from the hall to the front room, feeling Lisa's steely glare at the back of my neck. I half expected my back to start melting off. I felt vulnerable walking in front of her; I quickened my step.

Time has no consequence for them. And they have all the time in the world.

She seemed rather aloof for the crappy state that Guy was in. I turned and watched her as she returned to the kitchen sink, which was overflowing with bubbles. She stuck her hands in it, looking them over as if she found a long, lost jewel.

"Thanks for letting me see him, Lisa."

"Oh, it's my pleasure."

"If you don't mind, can I come over tomorrow? Just to see how he's doing?"

"That will be fine, Brooke. You have a wonderful afternoon now."

I felt like I was in a scene out of the Stepford Wives.

And was glad to let myself out the door.

Wonderful, my butt. The whole time I spoke with her, her eyes never left that sink of bubbles. Calgon had taken her away.

Great, if food poisoning looked like that, then I was a millionaire.

LYLE MCCORMICK

*L*yle McCormick thought he was seeing things. Either that or he was coming down with something. Or Ms. Cassie Dupree was spiking his food. Or maybe it was a combination of all three, but he hadn't drank all that much, had he? He brought a couple of beers with him on the boat. And he did bring a lunch; it wasn't like he drank on an empty stomach.

The morning started out pretty regular, at least for him. Cassie was sawing logs so loud he thought he heard the windows rattle. That woman was as loud in sleep as she was when she was awake. He had already been up the last hour before the alarm went off at precisely 4 am. He got up and splashed cold water on his face. He needed to rouse himself up and get a move on. It had been a restless night, and Tootles was on edge too. But Tootles could get flustered when the wind would blow.

After getting a pot of coffee going, he walked outside to his shed where he kept all his fishing equipment and picked out a last-minute piece of tackle. He walked back into the house to the smell of coffee permeating throughout the kitchen. After buttering his toast and savoring that first sip of liquid goodness, he eased back into his chair and took a few moments to admire the quiet. He loved that. It was just like being out on the lake.

He went over in his mind about where he would fish first. Of course, it would be his favorite spot, the little out of the way place that was ripe with fish of all sizes. And it was just steps away from Carver Island. It took a little bit of patience to get there with his small boat, but that was ok. Mainly because it was still a bit native and only people who grew up around here knew about it. He made a mental note not to forget his binoculars.

There was a young eagles nest high up in one of the old trees that sat like a fortress in front of it, and the momma had babies not too long ago. It was always a treat for him if he could spot them high up in the nest.

After getting his boat loaded up, he untied it from the pier and started up the motor. He liked early mornings like this. The lake had set a moody scene, there was steam-fog all around him. But he could get there with his eyes closed. He turned the light on in the front of his boat so he could easily be seen. Lucky for him, he knew about all the stumps in the area. A stump could kill a boat motor quicker than anything; he learned that the hard way over the years.

The spiky chill woke Lyle to his senses. He was haggard from the night before from no sleep. Despite that, he would still enjoy this. He hadn't been to Carver in ages. He liked how untouched the thickets and trees were there. Determined to get there in under an hour, he kicked the motor in full speed and headed north.

Several hours passed, and Lyle had a very productive morning. His boat was full of fish. And despite all the cleaning that he would be doing, he still doubted himself.

Not his fishing skills, they were spot on. He had caught plenty of fish, enough in fact that his deep freeze would be overflowing with them. He and Cassie would be eating fish for months.

No, he was doubting what his eyes were showing him. Even now he was trying to explain it away, making some sort of logical sense to it. But no matter how many times he ran it through his head, he came up with the same conclusion; and none of it made sense.

And no, he wasn't drunk. Two beers could hardly make one pie-eyed. And he had eaten more than a sensible lunch. Cassie had packed his roast beef sandwich so thick he could barely get his mouth around it.

Maybe his mind was playing tricks on him because he was in the first stages of Alzheimer's.

That wasn't too farfetched a thought. His uncle had passed away from it when he was a boy. His unfortunate end would always lie fresh in his mind, like a repeated bad dream. And it would probably always be.

His very bright and vibrant uncle had been reduced to spending long afternoons staring out the window in his favorite easy chair. He had taught Lyle how to fish, play cards, swim the lakes, getting girls, and just the general know-how of how to navigate through life. What was he now? The best he could muster was a heap of living mush. In Lyle's mind life delivered a cruel joke to his uncle. Where all that vitality, charm and intellect went was anyone's guess, and Lyle hated the scant, ripped up pieces that were left. He didn't know why he still visited him all those times; he might as well been visiting a tree. This hardened him. It was so undignified and cruel. And one of the worst injustices that life could deliver.

And Lyle would make sure that he wouldn't experience anything like that again. Period.

The only other scenario Lyle could come up with was maybe he had dreamed the whole thing up, bumped his head and hallucinated. I guess he couldn't rule it out, except what did he bang his head on exactly? He would have known if he did that. Lyle was too sharp a person not to remember. No, he didn't bump his head.

Whatever was lying out in front of him, all stretched out like a creature from the Black Lagoon didn't look of this earth. But it did look wise. And that it flew out of a page from a mythical tale. The kind that came in books that were thick as the bible and pages that were misshapen and discolored. Could dragons really roam the earth and breath fire? Was there really the lost city of Atlantis and mermaids that frolicked on the beach?

The closer Lyle got to this thing; it made him realize that seeing was indeed believing. But the question was, what was he seeing? The first thing he noticed was how big he was. It was massive and looked to be at least 12 feet long; and in one solid color: jet black.

If ravens were that big, it was the closest he could think of to compare. But he had a man face. A very long, tall man with a set of wings. And one was flapping about on the ground like it was broke.

Lyle got out of his boat to take a closer look. He waded through the shallow water near the thing and docked it. His shoes and pants getting soaked in the process, but he could have cared less. All he wanted to do was tie that boat to a tree. He remembered to take his rifle with him and had never been so happy in his life that he had brought it.

Just standing near it had Lyle on guard, he could feel the gun shake in his hands. He quickly took the safety latch off; his trigger finger ready. It was mortally wounded, and the tangy smell of blood was in the air. And it was smeared all over the place, amongst the reeds and on top of the surrounding grasses.

Seeing all this blood made Lyle momentarily dizzy. Whatever this was, it had been in quite a fight. Without thinking, Lyle bent down to get a closer look at its face. He didn't want to touch or disturb it, he just wanted to know what it was.

As he did, the thing sensed him and opened its eyes. He jumped at that; he was surprised it was still alive, with all the blood everywhere. And the eyes were larger than an average person, the whites of them stark against the color of his pupils, which were more merlot than red.

Lyle fought through his nervousness at the sight of those eyes. To look into them made you feel a great deal unsettled, but he couldn't divert his eyes. There was an alluring quality about the dark creature that Lyle had to tell himself to look away. He looked over its massive set of wings. He didn't know how, but he took his finger off the trigger and mustered up enough courage to run his hand across the top of its massive wing. It was soft as a dove. His other wing was still flapping, and looked like it was broke.

It took all of Lyle's will to ask it a question. But he just had to.

"Who are you?"

The thing seemed to want to respond, but it was an effort.

"I am, Avalone."

"What happened to you?"

The thing was on its last breath. His features looked pronounced and aggressive. He could also see deep cuts in its skin. Lyle couldn't help but feel sorry for it.

He felt like it was trying to read his soul.

"Your uncle.."

Lyle perked up.

"Yes?"

"Faded into the grey."

Lyle couldn't believe his ears. How the hell would he know about his uncle?

"What are you saying?"

Lyle felt like he was on his first day at school, and he was the young child asking silly questions, one on top of the other. And he also wanted to help it.

"Can I help?"

Maybe it was the humanity in Lyle, but he felt pity for this creature. Who knows what it had done, or what evil it was trying to do, he just never had the stomach to see anything suffer. But whatever had happened to it; it was beyond anything he could do. They both knew that.

"Who did this?"

"Aaron."

It was the last thing it spoke. The creature slowly closed its eyes for the last time. Lyle instinctively checked his pulse at the wrist, which he was surprised to know that despite its birdlike body, his arm and wrist looked human, except with longish type nails. He felt like he was looking at something dressed in costume.

He half expected the wings to come off. Lyle didn't feel comfortable touching or trying to move the thing. There was no more he could do for him now. And like a robot, he picked up his rifle, untied the rope from the tree and got back into his boat.

The boat started up right away, and Lyle was grateful. And all he wanted to do was hall-ass straight out of there. He took a quick glance back and could still see a little bit of Avalone, amongst the trees. From this vantage point now, he just looked like a big crow.

It wouldn't be long before the creatures from the island would devour him.

What Lyle just saw couldn't be explained in any rational sense. He hadn't lost his mind, hit his head, or had any sort of psychological break. No, this couldn't be explained away by logic or science. This would be something that would stay with him forever. He felt a little remorse because he knew he wouldn't be telling another living soul anything about it. He couldn't.

He only hoped there wasn't more of them.

INFESTATION

I could see Guy and Lisa walking up to the pool. They both looked chipper.

Wasn't Guy on his deathbed just a day ago?

But today was different, and so was he. He even walked a little differently. And he looked like he hadn't slept for a good two days solid. So, whatever was going on with him seemed to have passed.

Right.

And I could not read either one of their minds. It was strange because I had no problem reading Guy's the day before at the grocery store, and last night, even though it read fuzzy. Maybe what I experienced the other day was just a fluke. Maybe when I saw him, had I just overreacted? Could it have been just food poisoning? I was glad he was better, I guess.

Lisa was just Lisa. She had always left me the impression that she was off kilter.

Guy came walking up to me with a boyish grin on his face.

"Saw that guy you were talking to a few days ago. Where did he come from anyway?"

So, he was back to his ever-charming self. I ignored his question.

"Well, you sure got better. What the heck happened to you?"

"What do you mean?"

"You're kidding, right? You looked like you were at death's door yesterday."

"Yeah well, I guess you've never had food poisoning before."

I was puzzled.

"Well, no. But, look...you really had me worried."

"Well, I'm sorry I worried you. But, I'm all better now."

But why did he tell me that I should leave?

I wasn't entirely convinced, but I didn't feel like arguing.

"So, that guy you were with last week?"

"Yes, Aaron?"

Why was he so interested or even care? He had Lisa.

"He's just a friend."

"I just never saw him around here before."

"Well, I only met him a few weeks ago myself."

And in no way would I tell him the circumstances.

"Ok. Just keeping my eye on you is all. You never know what could end up being trouble."

"I know Guy, but he's perfectly fine."

If he only knew. It was kind of funny that Guy could get so riled up over Aaron. But I couldn't lie, it felt good to have him notice. It meant that he actually still cared, which was nice.

Lisa came walking up. She looked like she wanted to say something.

"Thank you for the food you brought over yesterday."

"Oh, no problem."

She walked over to the edge of the pool, dipping her toes in.

Guy was standing near, eyeing me strangely.

"Hey, I think I'm gonna try to catch something tonight if you want to go fishing later."

Fishing with Guy would be a much-needed diversion.

"Is Lisa coming?"

"Not really her thing. I think she just wants to relax with a book."

"Oh, ok."

Good. I didn't mind that at all. As we stood there, I was surprised to see Penny a couple of yards away. She walked by the pool and again wearing one of her heavy printed dress which could have easily passed for drapes. She was probably roasting in this heat but who was I to say. Penny looked in our direction and decided it was best to walk the other way. This seemed to be a pattern with her. She didn't seem to like being in our company.

While walking back to the house, I thought it odd how I couldn't read Guy's mind at all. I had tried several times during our conversation, but it didn't work. I had been able to read it while he was in bed sick. But now that he had gotten better, no luck. And not that this mattered, but I still couldn't read Lisa's either.

As I saw Guy walk down to the dock in his faded jeans, ripped up shirt and canvas shoes I remembered why I first had a crush on him in the first place. He was always so put together and cute. The kind of guy that made you feel safe standing next to. Well, that was until I met Aaron. It made me happy that maybe Guy was a little jealous. It made me feel good, and I so wanted to tell Guy what was going on around here. But every time I wanted to, Aaron's words echoed in my mind.

You cannot tell anyone.

Of course, I wouldn't, but it was hard. Things were getting stranger by the minute. I didn't know how Aaron thought I could hold that kind of secret without going crazy.

I wouldn't tell Guy anything of course. But I needed to know what he saw. Maybe distractors were already in Chicago. Perhaps he would tell me about what he meant by getting away.

Undoubtedly Guy was a safe person. I never felt threatened around him. I knew him since I was a young girl.

I remember one time I had swam too close to the deeper end of the pool; I had wanted to get a beach ball that was just out of my reach. I had slipped, and got a mouthful of water as I went under. I was a good swimmer, but for some reason, I was struggling. It wasn't long before I felt two strong hands bring me up out of the water, and carried me to the shallow end of the pool.

As I stood in the sun coughing up water, he was there beside me, with the sun on his face asking me if I was ok. I was shaken up, but ok. I was never so happy before to have him there. He had patted me on the back, gave me a little grin, and went back to the deep end of the pool with his friends.

I stayed there at the shallow end of the pool for the rest of that day. I would never forget that moment. He had been paying attention, and he had saved me. Other adults were around, but they weren't watching. But he did. From then on, I always thought of him as my knight and shining armor.

Guy had brought down a white bucket full of minnows. The bucket was heavy, but he carried it with ease.

He seemed anxious to get to some fishing. He had brought his large tackle box which looked to have every sort of lure possible, and in all colors and sizes. Well, it's not like he had any kids yet to spend his money on.

I looked out at the water and the sky. We were standing on my favorite dock, and tonight the sky was lit up in different shades of purple.

"You know what they say, 'Red night, sailor's delight. Red morning, sailor's warning.'"

"So, we're ok then."

He looked over and winked. I could hear the sounds of other fishermen across the lake. We weren't alone. Not that I was afraid or anything. But I couldn't shake off the strange feeling of the other day, and how awful he looked.

"Guy, I've been meaning to ask you, what did you mean yesterday by saying you saw something?"

He casted out and watched the bobber in the water.

"What do you mean?"

"You know, when you were sick in bed? You didn't look so great when I came to visit. And you mentioned that there was something here that was dangerous."

He started laughing.

"Dangerous, really?"

I stood there in disbelief.

"Yes."

"When did I say that?"

"Yesterday! When you were sick! Hello, you don't remember?"

"Well, I think I would remember saying something like that."

Great. He was going to deny it.

"Do you remember anything about being sick?"

My heart felt like it was pounding out of my chest. I was going to have to get control because he was really kind of pissing me off.

"Well, I know I ate something that didn't agree with me, and well, now I'm feeling better."

Ok, so let's just take you away with the other robots and hope maybe a toy store will buy you.

I talked slower because I wanted to make him understand.

"Guy, I know you ate something that didn't agree with you. But you said you didn't think it was safe for me to be here. You said it! You don't remember?"

I wished Aaron were here.

I watched Guy put his hand in the water, moving it like a lure in the water.

"How's the temperature?"

"Kinda cool, but nice."

A few fish gathered near his hand.

"So, you're a fish whisperer, too."

He didn't look quite himself then. Like he wanted to respond, but decided against it.

"They aren't even swimming away."

He grabbed one and took it out of the water. It was a bluegill, the large blue dot on it looking like a blueberry. He made a weird whistle, and the fish lay still in his hands.

"What did you just do? It's not even moving."

He didn't answer me, but knelt down. The fish still resting in his hand.

"I think you put him to sleep!"

I bent down to look and noticed a strange mark on the back of his neck.

"Guy, did you..."

I stopped mid-sentence.

No, no, no. This couldn't be. Why was this taking me so long to figure out????

Because I didn't want it to be true.

He let the fish slip back into the water. It darted away quickly. He turned his attention to me.

"What's wrong?" He looked alarmed.

"I've just never seen fish do that before, that's quite something."

I didn't remember Guy ever having a tattoo. He was probably already one of them. I always remembered Guy smelling fantastic. Today he smelled a little like hot garbage juice. Ok. Time to calm down. My imagination was in high gear. Maybe he just forgot to shower. People do that. It's ok.

But I couldn't shake it.

He was one of those things, a monster. I knew it.

Penny was right!! I had to get to her.

All I could think about was Aaron's voice lingering about, a heated whisper in my ear.

'*They are cunning, and they are smart. And time does not matter to them.*'

"I think I got a stitch in my side, it really hurts."

I needed to get out of there.

"You gotta get up and stretch once in a while."

He stood up and stretched his long, whitish arms to the sky. He wasn't near as tan as he had been the entire summer. It was that same sickly shade he had while lying in that bed. Except now it appeared to look more menacing too, if that was possible. Any moment now I half expected his Guy cover to come off, ripping at the seams, and out would step the real monster that he was.

Whatever you do, do not ask him about what you have seen on the back of his neck.

I started shaking. I so wanted to ask him. I was going to have to learn to control my emotions. That was another thing, Aaron said always to be aware of your surroundings and to control your feelings. I kept thinking how dogs could smell fear. If that's true, then Margie's dogs were smelling mine right now two miles down the road. They were probably having a field day right now down at the bar. I wondered if Guy could smell my fear. The thought made me nauseous. He probably could. I figured out that I was going to have to pretend my way out of this.

Aaron's voice rang in my ears again.

Just get out of there.

Again, I'm that girl in the fourth grade. It's my third day in, and I'm so nervous about making new friends at school, that I wasn't paying attention to the first step of the endless staircase from the top floor. I knew right away I was going to fall since I tripped over the first step, and I tried to brace myself for the long way down.

This was gonna hurt.

There is nothing like a good fall to humble a person. The teacher had raced up to me with a pained look on her face asking me if I was ok. Well, no. You try rolling like a log down a flight of steps.

"What's wrong, girl?"

He looked so innocent standing there. I searched his eyes for anything alien-like. Maybe if I stared long enough, I could start to see a little bit of the monster. Or perhaps a portion of his eye that might have been red. Like maybe his eyes had turned differently sometime during the night.

Nope.

They were still the same eyes, puppy dog brown. And I didn't see a hint of anything amiss, or even red eyes. In fact, I almost felt a little ridiculous.

Oh, how I very much wanted to not believe it.

Except Aaron was very real.

So was that thing with the red eyes.

And that darn tree.

And well, I couldn't deny my new 'supernatural' gift. Which for some reason, didn't seem to be working now with Guy. Maybe it was broke. I guess even supernatural powers could be unreliable.

Part of me wanted to give Guy a big hug and confide everything to him. I so wanted his tattoo to be real, with no hidden sinister meaning. I could feel my eyes filling with tears.

"Darn contacts. Think I got something in them. I hate that."

"Well, I lucked out in that department. Perfect 20/20 vision."

"Listen, I think I need to take these out, I'll be right back, ok? Need a soda or something?"

"No, thanks."

"Ok, I'll be right back."

I quickly walked up the dock towards the house. I wanted to scream, hyperventilate, anything. I ran in the front door and grabbed a glass out of the cupboard. I ran the tap until it was ice cold. It felt good running down my parched throat. I gulped down another glass. Thank goodness for simple water.

THINK. What now?

My mind raced.

Those numbers on the back of his neck....

So what, he got a tattoo, not a big deal.

He lives in the city. Aaron said they try to get as many people as they can, but without being too conspicuous. Maybe they knew he came up here. Who did this to him? Obviously it was when he was sick.

Another shiver ran through me.

No one else was home, thank God. Patti was at a friend's. Both parents were working. Mom was doing laundry in the middle of the resort. I ran up to my room.

What am I possibly going to do now? I can't go down there again. I won't. And who around here is doing it? This means Lisa is one of them, too. I tried to think of what Aaron would say.

You can do it. Act like nothing has changed.

My own pep talk wasn't winning me over. I walked over and looked out of our window that looked over the lake and piers. He was still there, just sitting on the bench. Like anyone else who would be sitting on a bench. Ok, I needed to get down there, or he would start to suspect something. But I didn't have to stay long. Just maybe a few minutes more. I could just tell him I was tired and wanted to make it an early night, he would understand that. I just hoped he couldn't tell when someone was pulling his leg.

I gathered my wits about me and walked back down to the pier.

"Hey."

"Your eye ok?"

"Yeah."

I tried to reel in my fishing line which was cast out. But I could feel the rod shake in my hands.

He's a monster, of the worst kind. And if he's anything like red eyes, you're in trouble. I probably should have just stayed in the house.

Was there any part of Guy still in him? I hoped to God there was.

"So, that guy I asked you about before? Where is he now?"

I could feel my face run poker hot.

Control your emotions.

Heart in throat.

Why did he want to know so much about Aaron? I immediately coughed up my soda. Nice. It trailed down the front of my shirt like a roadmap. Of course, he would want to know about Aaron.

"Umm, he's visiting friends. He'll be here soon."

And not near soon enough.

Trying to wipe soda off my shirt was useless.

Guy shook his head.

"That's good, but I wouldn't want him getting his way with you or anything."

"Having his way with me? Oh Guy, please, that's nothing to worry about."

Now, normally that would be funny. I longed for this to be just a figment of my imagination. It would just be so much easier. But there is no dreaming of that tattoo, his garbage smell, or his over-fascination with Aaron. And Lisa was already one of them. Deep down, I knew. Penny knew it, too. I should really start to give that girl more credit.

"I'm thinking about getting a tattoo."

I just blurted it out. Just like that. And I was one step away from losing it.

"Really? Are you sure about that?"

"Yeah, I don't know, something interesting, not anything cliqued or done a hundred times, like a butterfly on the shoulder. I want something a little bit different."

"Well, I happen to like butterflies." He said with an eerie grin. "Would your parents approve?"

"I don't know. When I'm 18, I pretty much can do what I want, right?"

"Good point."

I wanted to ask him so bad if he had one. I don't see how me asking would put anyone in danger. It's a standard question, isn't it?

"Hey, you don't have any do you?"

"No, not really for me."

I tried to hide the big, dumb look on my face.

Oh no.

"You should watch out for Aaron, though. Guys like that are only looking for one thing."

"I don't think he's that way, Guy."

"Well, what way would you call him then?"

His tone was short, and his demeanor changed, just in those couple seconds.

This isn't happening.

I had to say this right. I had to say this right.

"I don't know, I just don't see him as being *that* kind of a guy. And he's been nothing but nice so far."

"Well, I'm still gonna keep my eye on him."

I bet he was.

I had to find concrete proof that he could be one of them, a plausible distractor. I saw the tattoo, and he's acting strangely. The thought made me shiver.

"You ought to come visit Lisa and me sometime. We have extra room at our place, it really would be no problem at all."

Why was he trying so hard to get me to stay with him? Alone, and in another city. Usually I would have jumped at the chance; even though I knew my parents would never go for it. However, everything has changed now. All I could see was Aaron.

"Yeah, that would be great. Say, maybe you and Aaron could go fishing together while you're here, you know, show him some of the good fishing holes."

"Yeah, I could do that. Wouldn't take him for a fisherman, though…"

I was trying to figure how I was going to get out of this one. I didn't want him to be suspicious of me. And I didn't want to be with him by myself for too long. I just didn't trust what I would say to him. There still was a chance that he was human, but I couldn't hide what I saw on his neck. Why couldn't Aaron be here? He would know right away. I had no idea about how to deal with these distractors.

I cast my line out and stood up waiting for a little bite on the bobber. I longed for any distraction.

"You seem a little upset. Are you ok?"

"I don't know, my stomach is a little upset, I think. Patti tried her best at making egg salad, I think it sat out too long."

I could use the excuse of food poisoning, too.

"Well, don't let me keep you. I'm going to call it quits here pretty soon. They don't seem to be biting tonight."

Maybe you'd have better luck putting your hand in the lake.

He gave me a devilish grin, and I wanted to shrink away.

Remember time to them is different than it is for humans. And they are very patient.

"See ya, Guy. Have a good night."

I hoped my voice wasn't too sing-songy.

"Good Night, Brooke. I hope you feel better."

"Thanks."

I was grateful to leave, it was hard trying to be nonchalant walking up the steps when I wanted to run like a firecracker.

Those things had finally gotten to him.

The tears were flowing now. Lisa had probably done it that night. Thinking about how she did it made me sick. Who was next? How many other people at the resort have already been turned? And what was I going to do with what I know? What could I do?

Aaron didn't give me anything to get in touch with him. No address, phone number, nothing. Not even a little clue of what direction he might have taken. Heck, for all I knew he was down at the bottom of some waterbed, swimming in tunnels to reach his home. I had no idea where his real home was, and in a way, I didn't want to know. The thought was overwhelming.

I looked up at the clock- 10:18 pm.

Guy and Lisa were most definitely distractors. And they were staying at our resort, in cabin five. It had the best view of the resort and was also the biggest cabin. And I was stuck lying on my bed, staring at the ceiling, wondering what on earth I could do about it.

So much for Aaron's theory that they wouldn't be around. And why the heck isn't he here yet? I couldn't help being angry at him for leaving me alone. This was dangerous, and I didn't know the first thing about how to fight them. And somehow in the span of things I had acquired something that scared the crap out of me. I knew it was very powerful, but I was darned if I knew how to use it properly or why I even had it.

I didn't want to step an inch outside my room, let alone outside. But as I sat feeling sorry for myself, I couldn't help but hear a repeated scratching at my outside window.

Great. Guy and Lisa had schemed up a plan and were now scratching at my window so they could rip my guts out.

I was convinced that they were out there. And Aaron was probably off in another dimension, while I was stuck in alien land.

Resting my head on a pillow was useless. The little noises and knocks at my window were not letting up.

Great. Another tree has decided to come to life. And its Medusa-like limbs were trying to open my window.

It would be a miracle if I ever slept again.

THE SISTERS

I decided to take a little peek out the window. It was dark as ink. But I could still make out two figures standing close to the oak tree that overlooked the lake. I was right in their line of sight.

Oh, wonderful.

If this was Red eyes or any of his creepy friends, my family and I were goners.

They clearly had seen me, and whoever they were, they were sauntering toward the bedroom. This wasn't good news for me. There was no way I could outmaneuver one distractor, let alone two. By the time I took another breath, they were already at my window.

"You must be Brooke."

And I had NO IDEA who they were. But both were female, and in human terms, gorgeous. The kind of beautiful that made you stare at first glance.

"Can I help you guys?"

"She's not that pretty," The taller of the two said.

The one that spoke had long, blondish hair with tinsel like streaks. She had her hands crossed in front of her as she eyed me up and down. She didn't seem the type to put up with a lot of nonsense.

"Don't be so rude Iris!!" yelled the other, who was just as attractive, but in a more demure way.

"I do apologize my sister has completely lost all her manners. Would you mind terribly in letting us into your room? We just need to speak with you is all, in a more private setting."

And what, I'm dealing with a pair of vampires now?

"What a ridiculous notion. The human has a vast imagination."

"Shut up Iris."

Well, one had a sour personality. Fine with me. And I probably would need to let them in, because in another minute Iris looked like she was ready to smack the crap out of me.

She spoke again.

"Can you please hurry up, either let us in or not. But we need an invitation before we can set foot in your dwelling. And by the way, we are not vampires."

"Oh, I didn't mean to think that…"

Oh crap.

I gave them the go ahead. At least they asked my permission. I still half expected them to turn into bats when they entered.

They didn't. But they both flew in through the window before I could change my mind. I didn't even think the curtains moved. After a few uncomfortable minutes of me watching them look the room over, the taller of the two spoke.

"Were sisters of Aaron."

This made odd sense, and I certainly could see the resemblance. Their eyes were also strangely lit. It scared me, but knowing they were related to Aaron made me so happy I wanted to yell.

"We came to see what all the talk was about."

It was Tinsel Hair again. She was hell-bent on putting me in my place, which was ok. If this was his sister, I didn't really care.

"I am Avery, and the mouthy one here is Iris."

Avery gave the room a once over and asked if she could sit down in my chair.

"Sure."

Iris preferred standing in the corner. That was ok, she could keep her distance. She made me nervous and wished I had something more on than a flimsy nightgown.

"Aaron has been talking with the tellers. He wants you to come for a visit to our lands."

This was good to hear, but I had no idea what they meant.

"Tellers? Who the heck are they?"

They looked at each other.

"Hasn't he said anything about where he's from?"

"In bits and pieces, but not really. When is he coming back?"

"Oh, he'll be back, but were more concerned about what's going on here, in your land. We already know that this whole area is saturated with them."

I hoped I was following them right.

"You mean distractors, right?"

"Of course, the distractors, silly. By the way, how do you like your newly acquired specialty?"

"Iris!" Avery yelled.

"You'll have to excuse my sister; she is not very versed in interacting with humans."

I looked at her in amazement.

"That's ok."

Anything they could tell me about my new 'gift' I was all for.

"Aaron did it. He wanted to give you an edge until he gets back. For the record, I didn't think such a powerful gift should be given away like that to a human."

"Well, I'm sorry, but I didn't exactly ask for it."

Avery smiled a little.

Iris thought of me as a lesser creature, like maybe how we thought of birds. Apparently I wasn't deserving of it, but I couldn't help but agree with her a little.

"It's mighty, and not to be played with."

"I'm figuring that one out."

Just being able to have the ability gave me the willies, but I could have just as soon not had it, either.

"Aaron will be here in the next day or two. It's taking him longer then he thought to get all the proper permissions from the higher-ups. And, he has a little explaining to do regarding, your gift."

I was so intrigued with questions, I didn't know which ones to ask first.

"Permissions, for what?"

Neither of them said anything right away. Iris was more preoccupied with a picture of a horse I had on my wall.

"I love these creatures here. I wish they had them on our planet."

"I'm afraid this whole thing with you has created quite a stir in our world. It's not what I would call…permitted."

"Oh."

"Nothing against you, but we are not really allowed to interact with humans. It's frowned upon."

Avery rolled her eyes.

"Shut up, Iris."

I felt like the cockroach about to be stepped on by a giant foot. I was on the lower line of species here.

"Every once in a while, they do make provisions. Anyway, Aaron would die if he knew we were talking to you. He just wanted us to watch over you, make sure those things stayed away. He kinda frowns upon us interacting."

"Well, I guess you blew that one to shreds."

Avery looked over at Iris, and I thought Avery was going to burst out laughing. Instead, she let out a smirk. Iris wanted to say something, thought better of it and offered up a smile instead. I didn't think she did that often, so I took that as a good sign. I couldn't read either one of their minds, thank goodness for that.

"Oh, you can't possibly read our minds, dear."

"Sorry, I didn't really want to."

"You're not a very good liar, either."

"Iris, knock it off."

"I just wanted a better look at her. It's always good to know who your brother is enthralled with."

I stood there with I'm sure the dumbest look on my face. So, Aaron thought I was enthralling. The thought made me smile.

Iris kinda reminded me of Lisa. She had a lot of the same traits: both cold, both beautiful. But being that she was Aaron's sister, I felt an obligation to be nice, whether I liked her or not. Maybe eventually she would warm up to me.

"How could Aaron possibly give me this gift?"

"It's not hard. We all have special powers of our own."

I didn't doubt that for a minute.

"I can make inanimate objects move."

"Stop interrogating her, Iris. I don't like it, and Aaron wouldn't, either."

Now, I was the one intrigued.

I gave Iris a look that said prove it. Without any hesitation, I noticed all my horse statues that had decorated my room and standing on my wall shelves was slowly moving up in the air, some galloping, others dancing about like they were alive. I was watching and staring. I expected to see strings or something, but no, they were just dancing by themselves about three feet in the air, some higher, all around my room. And the only thing making them move was Aaron's edgy sister, Iris. She was watching them too, looking quite pleased with herself.

A couple of my dolls that always had homes on top of my comforter had started to float up to join the party. Some were turning their heads, others moving their arms and feet. To see this was not something for the faint of heart. It was very unsettling. Avery must have noticed by the look on my face.

"Iris, you've made your point, you can stop now."

"Whatever."

And with that, all my horse statues and dolls fell to the ground with little thuds. As I bent down to pick up the dolls, I was thinking that I was never going to be able to have them in my room again if I ever planned on sleeping. I hoped to God my parents didn't hear anything.

"Help her, Iris."

Iris just stood there, while Avery bent down to help pick up the last three horse statues. She tried her best to position them back on the shelf.

"It's ok."

"Please excuse my sister; she has the manners of an ogre."

"My sister can make fire."

Avery looked quickly at me and shook her head no.

"Don't worry, she wouldn't light your room up or anything, but she could if she wanted to."

Well, that made me feel so much better.

Avery gave Iris another look, and Iris grew quiet after that. I, however, wanted to know more about Avery and fire.

"Can you really?"

She shook her head yes like she was embarrassed. And a few seconds later she had produced a live fireball in the palm of her hand. She was tender and cupped it as if she were holding a fluffy kitten. Her skin was burning, yet it wasn't even turning red. She just stood there with a delighted look on her face.

The flames lit up her features, making her look ethereal. I couldn't help but be a little envious. I impulsively put my hand near it, just to feel the heat. And sure enough, it was hot enough to scorch a mere mortal's hands.

Having fed into my curiosity, Avery turned off the fire as quickly as it came. When it was out, she rubbed her hands on her leg a little and shrugged her shoulders, as if she just got done taking out a dirty bag of garbage. I expected her hands to show some signs of what happened, but of course, they weren't. I turned them over as I looked at them in amazement. Nothing was charred or black, just a tannish white.

To say this was magical was a gross understatement.

"That's my fire."

There was a lingering burning smell in the air, and that was it.

"That's amazing."

Avery smiled, more concerned with the business at hand.

"Did you say someone here is one of them?"

"Yes. Well, at least I think so. The couple staying in cabin five."

I cringed when I said that. I felt like a traitor to Guy. But at the same time, I didn't want him or Lisa going on some killing spree on the resort. Deep down I knew he was one of them.

"It was only a matter of time."

Tinsel didn't mince words. And I didn't like that she was ahead of the game for reading my mind.

"But you sure got a charge out of reading those innocents at the store, didn't you?"

Well, darn it.

"Leave her be, Iris."

"Oh, he's a distractor all right. I can smell them. There's at least two here at the resort. But don't worry, we will take care of it."

"What are you going to do?"

I might have well taken Guy to the firing squad. An image of him popped into my head, all feeble and sick. Depressing.

But he was already dead.

"I know you guys are used to all this, but I had just learned about all of you a month ago, and I'm afraid I'm not used to it yet."

Iris let out a laugh.

"She's funny Avery. I kind of think I enjoy talking with these humans. Maybe we should do more of it."

"We should do none of the kind, Iris."

She turned her attention to me.

"We will take a look in the area. But if they have suspected that you already know they will have already left. Besides, they weren't planning on invading your planet for another forty some odd years."

I didn't quite know how to process what Avery just said. But my first question was, how the heck would she know?

"We know. Trust us on that one."

They both said their good-byes and assured me that we would end up seeing each other again, but they couldn't tell me when. I felt that I had an ally with Avery. Iris on the other hand, well time will tell. But for now, she just scared me.

While they were off scouting around the resort tracking down Guy and Lisa, (and how they would do that was anyone's guess), I was back to the quiet of my bedroom. Our little visit didn't wake up anyone else in the house, and I was glad for it.

I didn't want to ask questions about what they would do, I was thankful they knew what was going on around here, and I got to meet a part of his family. I was excited as ever to know that he would be coming back here soon.

As much as I wanted to stay awake and worry about all that was going on, my body was craving sleep. I was beyond exhausted, and I wasn't going to be of good use that way.

Before I could drift off, I had to take the three dolls that I've had forever in the corner of my room and carry them down the hallway into the closet. And that's where they would be staying. I went back to bed, and let sleep take me to where it wanted to go. In my dreams, I thought I may have seen Guy. His eyes were bright and dazzling, and he looked to be in a much better place.

I didn't know how long I was going to last playing the waiting game and pretending everything was perfectly normal, when it wasn't.

Sleep wasn't something I could do for long periods anymore. I kept thinking of distractors roaming about out in the woods, or who knows where else. I double bolted the doors at night and left a night light on in my room. I hadn't needed one of those since I was a little girl. But these were desperate times. And I always did a running check of my family before retiring to my room.

Aaron had once explained that their main thing right now was to stay hidden in the shadows. They weren't going to reveal themselves anytime soon. But I was still a jumble of nerves.

ETHEL WATSON

*E*thel was enjoying her morning cup of coffee while peering out her window at the lake. Her house was about a quarter mile down the road from Cassie's. It looked like it was going to be a pleasant day, despite the morning chill in the air.

Ethel liked to get her swim done early when the fog still rested on top of the lake. She liked swimming through it; it always gave her the sensation that she was doing something very out of the way and dangerous. But there was never anything dangerous at the lake, the only thing you had to worry about is knowing how to swim.

Afterward she would have the rest of the day to do what she liked, which was shop and do a little gossip with Cassie, of course. She had gotten into this routine years ago. It just made her feel a lot better. She loved the rush she would get, feeling the coolness of the lake water against her skin.

Ethel liked that her skin never looked old under the water. The wrinkles seemed to disappear like it was dipped in magical liquid. No one was out at that time, and it was nice having the lake all to herself.

Once in a while there would be a tenacious fisherman or two, but their boats usually clung around the edges of the lake, staying close to the bogs and lily pads, where fish liked to settle in groups.

She figured she was pretty safe doing her laps to the other side and back. And boats didn't come out there usually until later in the morning anyway.

After getting her one-piece floral suit and swim cap on, she found her way down to the dock. One thing about the North Woods, it was easy to like and so darn beautiful. The fine morning mist hung just a few inches above the surface of the water; and it was oddly beautiful. She could hear loons overhead.

It was going to be a chilly swim. But she was determined to get one more in before fall decided to settle in on Neelsville. She carefully tiptoed in, like she always did, which was the hard way. As she inched closer, she smiled thinking of what Cassie might say, 'Gotta just jump in girl, not gonna get used to it that way.'

Ethel wondered what Cassie might be up to today. She would have to give her a call. They were always doing something together in the summertime. She finally got herself right up to her neck and treaded water for a bit to let the temperature of the water get comfortable with the rest of her body. She would do this for a little bit before starting the long trek across the lake and back.

It really wasn't that far to the other side. Maybe 30 yards? She had done it a hundred times. But somehow something about this morning felt a little different. She couldn't put her finger on it, but it had nothing to do with the weather. She had noticed it while sipping her coffee at breakfast. When she looked out over the lake, it seemed a little different, but she brushed it off as a passing thought.

Up ahead she noticed a few bubbles brewing up from the lake below. This didn't startle her because it wasn't unusual to see. There was a lot of turtles that occupied the lake, and she didn't pay the fish any mind, and they never paid any mind to her. Sometimes she would see a turtle coming up, but it would be rare to see one right there in the middle of the lake. They usually liked it more toward the shore.

But there were more now. There were bubbles all around her; like she was in the middle of a brewing coffee pot. Funny, she didn't remember a spring being under there....

She altered her swim path a bit and continued on with her lap.

As she continued, she felt the slightest pass of something brush across her lower leg. She couldn't help but yell out.

"What was that?" she yelled to no one particular.

Her voice echoed across the water and caused a flurry of birds to fly off the tops of the trees.

She felt for her foot. It was still in one piece. She sighed in relief.

She quickly brushed it off, thinking that she would be brushing off whatever touched her. There was seaweed floating all through the lake. It was probably some of that.

She continued on with her swim. She was just getting into her groove when she noticed something swirling about right in front of her.

It looked like someone was about to emerge right there in the water.

At first, she thought she imagined it.

"Hello."

She almost plowed right into him.

"WHAT?" she said in a bewildered state.

She first noticed the white contrast of his skin. His face had emerged from the lake with an odd like smoothness. A ghastly smile crossed his face like he was the alligator that just swallowed a poor, unsuspecting animal. The colored coffee droplets of lake water were in stark contrast to his white face. They slowly trickled down his cheek and his long, pointed nose.

It was baffling to her what she was seeing. His head had just popped up out of the water like a wine cork.

She watched as one droplet of water lingered on the end of his nose. The smile left his face, and now he didn't have any expression. But his cool blue eyes held her stare, and they were searching hers. She almost felt like he was trying to get into her head.

This left Ethel feeling cold, and it wasn't from the morning water. She still treaded water a few feet from him. His face looked familiar....she searched her mind...of course, at the picnic.

"Guy?"

"Yep, that's me. Guy."

Somehow Ethel wasn't entirely convinced. There was that creepy grin again. Like he had just told a bad joke. She shuddered.

"How? Well, how are you here? I didn't see you get in."

"I swam, my dear."

She turned around and looked back at the shore, trying to figure out where he could have gotten in. The resort was a good four miles in the other direction. Something about him wasn't jiving. But then again, she was here swimming, too.

"You, um, startled me."

"That's a fetching swim cap if you ask me. But truthfully, that thing could scare all the fish in town."

She was wearing her lime green one. Usually she would have thought that funny. Now, not so much.

"Well good. I don't care much for fish."

She watched as his face took on a more sinister tone.

"I'm just here enjoying the water. The real question is, what are you doing?"

This made her back up. She hated him invading her space like this. This was her time, her territory, her lake. And he was just a guest at Fish-A-While. Funny she even recognized him at all, his face seemed to change subtly before her eyes with each moment. He was different, but yet the same.

"I didn't see you come into the water."

She watched as he decided how to answer.

It also smelled like something was rotten in the air. It seemed to be coming from him. A wicked smile reached his lips.

"Excellent idea, swimming. How long have you been doing this?"

"Awhile, I guess."

Why would he care?

Instinct had her backing up. He was getting too close for comfort.

"I love it."

She decided to act a little more cordial; maybe he would leave sooner.

Ethel looked behind her. The shore was still a good 50 yards away. She could try and make a run for it. It might have well been a thousand miles away.

"It's good for the soul."

Something itched in her. This Guy thing, whatever it was, looked like he didn't know much about a soul.

She needed to get out of there, quick.

"I better finish my laps, I'm kind of in a groove."

She didn't wait for a reply. She went around him and continued on, catching another glance before swimming away.

The look on his face made her wish she had on a jetpack.

She could hear him talking as she tried to get more distance between them.

"I just wanted to ask you something about your friend Cassie."

He was toying with her now.

She had a good twenty feet start, and she felt herself swimming faster.

"I just want to talk to you is all. Are you scared of a little small talk?"

She could feel him almost at her heels.

Oh dear lord, he was following her. And he wasn't following her because he wanted to talk.

She swam and swam like her life depended on it.

She knew that now.

All her splashing was probably scaring all the fish in a 10-mile radius. She didn't care. She only hoped that someone on shore could see or hear what was going on. She kept up with her long strokes. She wasn't going to look back. She didn't want to waste any more time.

Her skin didn't care or even feel the temperature of the water now. Was it warm or cold? She didn't know. She couldn't seem to feel anything. The only thing she felt was panic…fear…adrenaline.

And dread.

She was almost there now, back to the safety of land. All she had to do was just get there already. Once on the other side, she would be able to get some help.

Just get out of the water.

Ethel kept swimming, and she was starting to wear thin. She was getting more and more out of breath. The lake's edge was so close now; soon her feet would be able to touch bottom. One thing she hated about this lake was it was always anyone's guess where the bottom was. She hated that. And wishing right now that she could at least see something.

She felt as if her lungs would burst if she went any farther. She quickly looked behind her and was surprised to see nothing. She stopped for a few seconds, trying to catch her breath.

The lake was calm, flat, and dark. Grey storm clouds was brewing overhead now. She could feel the rain in the air.

She frantically looked around, and around. Was he indeed gone?

"Guy?" She said in a nervous voice.

Before she could say anything more, she felt something grab at her ankle and pulled her down into the lake.

The heavy hand felt like an anchor, and she knew instantly she was in trouble.

She held her arms out in front of her flaying and trying to grasp at something, anything to help pull her up.

She concluded that this was going to be futile.

Knowing this, she said several prayers and closed her eyes until it was over.

HE'S BACK

A knock on my bedroom window stirred me awake. I had only been asleep a couple of minutes; that was the running tally these days. I opened my eyes to see Aaron staring at me from outside the window, and I couldn't get out of bed fast enough. I popped open the window thinking that if I took too long, he would vanish into thin air and I would wake up from my lovely dream.

"I've missed you." He whispered in my ear and brought up his hand which he lightly caressed my cheek. It felt like heaven.

"That's likewise. You were gone so long, I was worried."

"I was worried for you, for everyone around here."

"When did you get back?"

A few hours ago.

"I met your sisters."

His eyes were blazing.

"My sisters? CAME HERE?"

"Why, yes they did."

"What did they say to you?"

"They just introduced themselves."

I thought I would spare him the floating dolls and fire story.

"They weren't supposed to talk to you."

"Well, don't be too mad at them. They were probably just curious."

"Were they nice to you?"

"For the most part."

"Even Iris?"

"Well, she was ok."

"I tell ya they can be a pain, but you want them on your side."

"I got that loud and clear. And by the way, when you were gone, I seemed to have acquired something."

He spun around and took me in his arms.

"I know. I was afraid for you. I wanted you to have a bit of an edge until I could get back here."

"Well, I had an edge alright."

"I can take it away if you want."

I thought about that. It was a pretty cool thing to have. Maybe it wouldn't be so bad to have it for just a little while longer.

"Just like that, huh?"

Well, I wasn't quite ready for that either.

"I wouldn't mind having it longer if that's ok with you."

He grinned.

"Ok."

I didn't want to hear bad news, even if it was from him. It was just nice to have him here sitting with me. I almost wanted to pinch myself.

Cassie came running up to my mom's house with a quickness that I have never seen before. She looked like her train had been off its track for awhile. Her skin was red and her eyes tired and puffy. Steaks of mascara were running down her cheeks. Her bleached out hair was sticking out all over the place. She was a quite a sight, and it was startling to see because Cassie was always so well kept normally.

Aaron hid in my room, while I walked up the stairs and met her at the front door.

"Oh thank heavens Christ, your home! Is your mother around?"

"No, she's not here now. What's wrong Cassie?"

She took a deep breath to compose herself. And another pregnant pause for good measure. Cassie always liked her pregnant pauses. She would have made a great actress.

"It's Ethel. Christ, I don't know what has gotten into her. I've rung her up several times, and she doesn't even answer her phone."

"Maybe she's just not home, you know how she likes her swims."

As I was saying this, I knew Ethel could be in trouble.

"Well doll, it is very unlike Ethel not to answer her phone. And I know she goes out for her swims, but that was hours ago, and usually, she always takes my calls. And if she goes anywhere, I'm usually the first to know it. The pathetic thing doesn't like to do anything without me. I always know where she is. I think something God-awful has happened to her. I can feel it. I can feel it in my gut. There is something wrong."

She brought her well-manicured hand to her lips, her eyes wide as saucers.

"Oh dear heavens, my cherries in the snow, I forgot my lipstick. Oh, darling, forgive me, I must look like a complete fright."

I couldn't help but smirk. Cassie was just so well, Cassie.

"No, you don't look a fright. Scared maybe. Do you want to come in?"

I felt like she shouldn't be alone.

"Oh darling, maybe a glass of water would be nice. I sure could use something stronger, but it's not 3 o'clock yet."

"3 o'clock?"

"Only drunks drink before 3 in the afternoon."

"Oh."

I let her in and told her to sit down. She helped herself to the kitchen cupboard and found a glass and filled it up.

"Oh, I just feel like I could faint. Please forgive me if I pass right out here on your hardwood floors. But, I'm really worried. Ethel usually picks up her phone."

"Well, maybe give her the morning. She might just be running errands. We could always go over there and check for you."

"Oh, would you doll? That would make me feel so much better. I don't want to go over there myself; I don't want her to think I'm spying on her or anything."

"Yeah, I can walk over there."

Cassie straightened her blouse and composed herself.

"Just, well I don't know. I don't quite feel like myself at all. Something fishy in Denmark around here."

She didn't know the half of it.

"Did you see something?"

"Just a particular feeling I get. Feels like I have to always look over my shoulder. Like I'm being watched or something. I don't know. You know I have a special sensitivity to all that."

I did know that. And Cassie was right on the mark; she did seem to understand things that others didn't. But like me, she kept that to herself. I wondered if she suspected anything about Aaron.

"Well, I haven't done this in years, but I'm gonna start locking my doors. When I get my itchy feelings, they usually come from a good source."

And with that Cassie Dupree quickly walked out the door. She quick stopped short and turned around.

"And Brooke?"

"Yes, Cassie?"

"Tell Barb to start locking her doors. I mean it! You, too. Be careful when you go out."

"I will, Cassie."

"And please, let me know if you find anything peculiar at Ethel's."

"Don't worry, I will Cassie."

"Thanks, Doll!"

I watched as she quickly walked back up the dirt path to her cabin, which was only a few yards away. Her silky chiffon blouse untucked and trailing in the wind behind her, leaving behind the faint smell of Channel No. 5.

"She's right you know."

Aaron's voice startled me. I turned around and saw the look of dread on his face.

"We should go to Ethel's house."

I was thankful that Pattie was in town at a friend's house, my dad was at work, but I was worried for my mom. I didn't want to leave her alone when that thing was at our resort.

"He's not going to hurt anybody in broad daylight. You know it wouldn't hurt to check out Ethel's house. I'll know if they've been there as soon as I step in the door."

I walked down into the canning room where mom was busy organizing dozens of cans of vegetables in neat little rows for the fall and winter season. It was never a room I particularly liked, it was always cold and dank, overcrowded, and had one long, dirty string that hung off the light bulb from the ceiling.

The room smelled earthy, and I couldn't stand it when mom wanted me to go down there to grab a jar of something by myself. The whole basement was creepy to me. Even though my room was off to the side of it, I had to walk through the basement to get to it. I didn't know how she could stand it being down there by herself.

"Hey, Mom."

"Hi, honey. I have lots of stewed tomatoes here. These will be nice to have right in the middle of a snowstorm."

I was glad Mom was going to be occupied with this for a while. Plenty of time for Aaron and I to go to Ethel's.

"Thought I heard someone at the door."

"Yeah, it was Cassie. She's a little worried about Ethel."

"Oh, really?"

She stopped placing the jars on the shelf. She had a small look of alarm on her face.

"What's wrong with Ethel?"

"Well, she can't seem to find her. And she hasn't answered her phone."

Mom returned to organizing.

"Could you hand me those cans please?"

I handed her the last three jars of tomatoes that were on the floor.

"Well, you know Cassie. You know how she likes always to dramatize things."

"I know. I just want to go out for a little walk through."

"Don't go too far. We have a few things to do before the party tonight."

"I know. Thanks, Mom."

I didn't give her a chance to change her mind. I quickly ran back up the stairs.

Ethel lives a short distance from our resort. Her house is set back away from her dirt road. It was a long, rectangular ranch. And the lake was practically in her backyard. I had been in her house on several occasions. It was nice except for the galley kitchen, which is a fancy way of saying 'cramped.' Ethel is single now; her husband died long ago. No need for a big kitchen and she liked the house too much just to sell it.

As I walked down Pony Road with the boy whom I was clearly taken with, I wondered how I could have gotten so lucky to have met him. What were the odds? I was so relieved that he was finally back I could barely stand it. Like my heart was ripped out and now was pleasantly put back in its place where it rightly belonged.

It was so nice having him here, walking beside him. I marveled at seeing him up close; it made my heart beat faster. And despite all the crazy things that were going on around us, I felt safer being around him.

I liked the smell of his cologne, or maybe it was just him. And despite all that was going on, all of it didn't matter when I was with him. I just couldn't believe that someone like him, this Greek god, actually liked *me*. Me, the way I was. I didn't even have to change in any way.

The thought of it was mindboggling and still made me wonder a bit sometimes even why. I knew in the back of my mind that he could always change his feelings for me, he may not always be around. But for now, I was ok with it. I had so many questions for him; I didn't know where to begin...and I didn't want to ask the wrong one. But I really needed to know. It was crucial to our relationship.

"So Aaron, where did you go?"

"I went to see family again. It was nice, it had been awhile."

He could be so quiet and distant. I didn't want to pry, but I asked anyway.

"Where is your home?"

"I told them about the distractors here. I told them about you."

"Oh."

I blushed.

"We are in danger. All of us. And we are going to have to figure out how to fight them."

"Oh, Aaron. This all seems so impossible. I don't even know if I would have believed you if I didn't see you at the lake."

"I'm glad you decided to go fishing, by the way, that night."

He held my hand as we quickly walked over to Ethel's. We decided it would be better if we didn't tell Cassie what we may discover. She was already upset. But it was going to be hard to pull one over on Cassie. But Aaron could tell a lot of things by just walking into a room. His warm hand held tightly to mine. It was nice, and I felt safe.

As we came to Ethel's house the wind was blowing dandelion fluff all around us, making it look like it was snowing in the middle of summer. Ethel usually kept her garage door open; most people did around here, so we were able to walk right in. I could feel Aaron had his guard up from the start. He walked into her garage and looked around.

"Well, someone's been in here alright."

A pair of mountain bikes were hanging up from hooks on the ceiling….some fishing tackle and poles….an old plastic baby gate. Aaron walked to the side door and softly knocked.

No answer.

No footsteps could be heard coming to the door. He opened it a little more and peered in.

"Ethel?" he said.

We walked in together. I felt funny walking into her house without her permission.

"This feels wrong, Aaron. Maybe we should leave."

"No" he said. He walked into the living room, looking around like a private detective.

"Someone's been here. It's all over in here, and it's not Ethel."

"Well, she's allowed to have visitors."

"Not visitors of this kind."

Aaron could smell the faint last remnants of an old earth. The tell-tale sign of *distractor*.

I stood there wondering.

"What do you sense, Aaron?"

"A distractor was here. Right in this house, and right in this room."

I felt panic.

"What? How?????"

Aaron looked around.

"Well, they found her alright."

"But, where is Ethel?"

"Ethel?" He looked towards my direction and shook his head no.

"What do you mean, Aaron? What happened?"

"I don't know, but Ethel is gone. And not alive, most likely."

"How can you tell that?"

Aaron quickly ran out to the deck and looked out at the water.

"Here, he killed her. In the water."

"How do you know?"

"Because I can see her energy. Her fear is still in the air a bit. It's circulating down there.

He pointed towards the middle of the lake.

"He killed her this morning. In another hour or so this trace energy will be gone. I'm sorry."

Tears welled in my eyes.

"Is this all my fault Aaron?"

Aaron quickly walked over to me.

"Of course not. They've been scouting out this place for years. They already knew about this small town. It's not your fault."

"But how can you tell, that she's gone I mean? How do you see her energy?"

"Well, it's pretty obvious. I can see fear and anger and happiness as tangible as you can see things.. like living trees and grass. Or I should say, I can read what their mind is truly saying."

"But why, and why out in the water?"

"Well, it's kind of a game to them, and they change their mind. The kill is the thrill for them, and they like to toy with people. Sometimes if they find someone or something fascinating or different, they may have an attack of consciousness and let them be. But that's rare. They are nothing but evil. And what they do allow to pass over, they end making up for and doing that much more evil.

Maybe he decided to leave Cassie alone that night. Maybe because he could come back and wipe out this whole town years later."

"What?"

This was getting to be all too much.

"What do they want with us? Why don't they just leave us alone? Aaron, where is Ethel?"

"I don't know where she is right now. But she's not herself anymore."

I started crying right there on Ethel's couch. Aaron put an arm around my shoulders.

"I would never let any of them hurt you or your family or any more of the good people in this town. Don't forget, we are pretty strong ourselves, ok?"

I wasn't convinced. Sure, I knew Aaron had powers of his own. That was evident with the tree, with his mind-reading. But Aaron was good, and these things were so, well horrible. Their trickery seemed impossible.

"Oh, we've got a few tricks up our sleeves as well."

He must have read my mind again. Great.

"Please don't do that."

"I'm sorry, Brooke."

"No, it's not you, I just can't believe this is happening right now."

"They like to catch people off guard. Because let's face it, there are many distractions to keep your minds busy. And it only gets worse as time goes on. There will be even more distractions."

I felt sick to my stomach.

"Listen, Aaron. I have to tell you something."

He looked alarmed.

"What is it?"

"I think um, I think Guy is one them."

"Why would you think that?"

He looked like he was about to panic.

"No why?"

"Because they can be fooled, but it's hard to do."

"You didn't tell him that you knew, did you?"

"No, I don't think I did."

"He just can't know. I'm surprised it didn't register with me that he was."

"I mean, I could be wrong Aaron, I don't know. He just seemed off when I saw him fishing the other day. And the fish, he did some weird thing, he put his hand in the water, and about three fish went right to it, like his hand, was a magnet or something."

Aaron gave me a questioning look. Then looked over at Ethel's TV.

Aaron concentrated on it, and it turned on just like that. Another thing that I had no idea he could do.

It was of course, on the news channel.

"The young man was walking home and said he was attacked by a vagrant dressed in costume like clothes. He kept saying that he looked, 'quite unusual' and 'not of this earth.' This young man was quite shaken up over the whole ordeal. Any information regarding this individual, please call the Lincoln County Police Department."

'Oh boy, it's just what I thought."

"You know that thing that attacked you?"

I wouldn't forget that in a hundred years.

"Yes."

"Well, it's attacking others. I'm astonished. Uusually this kind of thing happens once every fifty years or so. Not multiple times in the same year."

I was puzzled then.

"What do you mean?"

Aaron looked like he wasn't sure how to say it.

"Look, just tell me what you know, Aaron. Please. I don't like being in the dark here, literal or otherwise."

Aaron nodded.

"Well, the thing that attacked you. They are much more powerful than a distractor. More powerful, because they are in control of the mayhem. They basically tell the distractors to do the dirty work for them. The problem is they can't hide beneath a facade. They are what they are. That's why they don't come out so easily, or in the daytime at all. They save themselves for the dark. They carry out their deeds that way. They are the ones that give out the numbers."

"What do you mean the numbers?"

"How many numbers of people are to be in accidents or mayhem I guess you call it, for the day."

"What? What do you mean? Do you mean there's someone in charge of all that? Accidents?"

"Well, sometimes things just happen. But sometimes it's the work of distractors."

I felt sick to my stomach.

"I've seen it. There are only a few of them. But there are thousands of distractors. The few of those red-eyed things give out the numbers of how many people are supposed to die on that day. And the distractors carry it out."

"My brother and I got captured by one. I couldn't even tell you where this was. It wasn't even on your planet or ours. But I saw what they did. He said 20,000... over there....And he points at the planet. At your planet, earth. And he's like communicating with them. They hear them, and they carry it out.

"You mean they say how many people are supposed to die on that day, and they carry it out?"

"Yeah."

I listened in horror at this impossible idea. I felt like I was in an alternative universe.

"But don't things just happen sometimes? Accidents?"

"Usually they are interested in larger groups. Although they may cause an accident if they had a particular vendetta against someone in particular."

"But how do you know it's them and not just horrible timing or something caused by Mother Nature or something?"

"They always leave clues. They enjoy it really, kinda like rubbing it in our faces."

Was any of this possible? I felt like I was in the middle of a fairy tale with a nasty ending. So, fairy tales could be true. I wanted to burn every fairy tale I ever read.

"I know this is a lot."

"How do you travel?"

I had wanted to ask him that since he got back.

"Well if you must know, it's usually underground, or through the water."

"Really? How?"

I was intrigued.

"We come up or down usually from a body of water. A pond, river, lake, ocean…it doesn't matter. As long as there's a form of liquid, then we can do it."

"Why do you need water?"

"Because it's everywhere, and it makes it easy for us to get back and forth."

"Do you have like, well, a spaceship?"

He laughed at that.

"We have a means of travel, yes. But something I can't show you right now."

"And, why?"

"Because it's not here. My brothers are using it. They are in my homeworld right now. I've told them what is going on here. And they are coming.

"When?"

"In a few weeks."

"And you'll go back with them?"

He paused.

"You know I couldn't leave you here with these 'things', around don't you?"

I sighed with relief.

"Good."

"But, could I ever go to your world?"

He stared at me for a long time.

"I don't know. I don't know if you would be compatible with our land."

"But they will be coming back, and we're going to have to fight them off."

"How?"

"The more of those we can kill, the better off it is for you, your kind."

"And we know how to find them. But we will have to teach you how."

"Human beings, you mean."

"Yes."

He stood and stared at me. I just liked staring into his beautiful eyes. They looked full of knowledge. Lovely pools. I could have stared at them all day.

Here we were at Ethel's house. And she was more likely dead or not herself anymore, which I felt terrible about. But at the same time, I wondered if he would kiss me right there in her living room. I felt like I wasn't much better than the distractors themselves.

"I told myself I wouldn't read your mind unless of course, you wanted me to." He whispered.

I looked away. I embarrassed easily when he looked at me that way.

"It's not fair that you can read my mind and I can't read yours."

"I know that."

To see him was okay, but there was still a small part of me that was scared of him.

Alien. Not of this earth.

"Are you scared of me, Brooke?"

"No."

There's a great big lie. I'm sure he could more than detect obvious bull crap.

I closed my eyes as I felt his breath caress my cheek. I waited to see what he would do. I preferred that he make the first move. But he didn't, he just whispered in my ear.

"You make me want to stay here. You make me want to help what's going on around here."

I felt his soft kisses leaving a trail up my neck. And then finally, his lips found mine. And I was carried away to a magical place, where the cares of the world were far away. My once grey world was starting to turn into different colors. After that, there's little hope of going back to the grey.

"I promise I will never let anything hurt you, Brooke, ever."

I believed it.

Aaron turned off the TV. We left Ethel's house just the way we found it. The only thing we left was the electricity of us. We closed and locked her door. I was just glad to be out of her house. It was a sad thought knowing that she would never step foot in her own home again.

Aaron never got a chance to see if Guy was a distractor because he and Lisa had checked out the night that Aaron's sisters had visited me. It was either that, or they had done something to them. It was a relief to me because I felt that he was already taken over as a distractor. And I was darn sure Lisa was one, too.

When he had first come to the resort, he seemed so normal, himself. There was nothing out of place. And my crush on him was still in full force. It seemed hard to believe that he was a distractor then. The whole idea was crazy. Was he just pretending to fit in then? I didn't know. Aaron said it was best that he did leave. There were distractors already permeating throughout the area and around the state. The only thing I could do now was just sit and wait.

And I felt incredibly useless.

BACK FROM THE DEAD

*C*assie was distraught. Most afternoons I could see her sitting on her porch, sipping her drink of choice from one of her canning jars. She said she liked sitting on her swing, that it made her happy. But lately, that's all she did. And she always wore the same thing day after day.

Ethel was missing. She had been gone now for three weeks. It's been three weeks since Aaron, and I were in her house, and he had noticed traces of Ethel in her backyard. This was a huge deal in our small town. Nothing like that had ever happened before. The police department was notified, and Cassie had put in a missing person's report. Police stopped by Cassie's home to investigate, and now Ethel's house was roped off with yellow crime scene tape.

There is a fine line between minding your manners and being a fighter. Sometimes it's hard to let your guard down. Because when you do, it usually comes back and bites you right back in the butt. You need to fight for everything in a sense, to breathe, to eat, to work, to make money, to acquire things, so you can live happily.

Nothing is ever free, and everything is a struggle. And for what? Who knows. It's not easy, nothing worth it ever is. And this new world that I had been let in on had all of these same things, except now it was only going to get harder.

I remember I could always see people for how they really were. Sometimes it was a gift, but usually, it was just an annoying curse. I could always tell if someone was giving me a line. And I felt that some could sense that too, and they despised me for it.

I remember my classmate Stacy Baker. She was pregnant her junior year. She decided to have the baby, and a bunch of us decided to visit her and her new little bundle. As soon as the baby touched my arms, I felt something. I don't know where it came from, but it was a voice that said, 'Not long for this life.' It wasn't like a loud voice I heard or anything; it was more of a feeling. And it was so resolute, and I had no idea where it came from.

A year later, her baby had died of pneumonia. After that happened, any odd feelings that I would get about someone, I ignored. It scared me because they usually came true. And I wanted to turn this extra sensory thing I had off. I didn't want it anymore.

I was terrified that maybe one of these things would find out about my abilities. Perhaps they would try and use me. I was scared that they would try and seek out my family. Aaron assured me that this wasn't going to happen, that they weren't ready yet. They couldn't really think for themselves unless they were personally under the threat of dying. But just the same, I felt very vulnerable.

Neelsville was buzzing around. You could hear the occasional firecracker in the distance every twenty minutes. Labor Day was coming, and you could smell the end of summer in the air. People liked to light up their fireworks long after the 4th of July. The city had an 11 pm ordinance, but of course, that was never followed or even really enforced.

The good kind of fireworks are illegal in Wisconsin, so a lot of people traveled to the Indiana border to get their firework stash.

And get some they did. Many liked to fire them off from their tippy row boats in the middle of the lake.

I was helping mom move picnic tables all in a row alongside the lake. They were having their end of summer picnic where everyone on the resort came and brought a dish to pass. They always ended up getting the sweet end of the deal, because my parents always had more than enough food, and entertainment for that matter. But the food was the farthest from my mind. In fact, I hadn't had much of an appetite lately. And I know it was from nerves.

All the dogs that lived around Pony road seemed to be in on the secret, too. Margie's included. It was rumored the bigger of the two which was Adam, would bite itself a lot. It now had a horrible rash on its body, and it looked infected. It kept to itself near Marjorie's feet on the other side of the bar. The other one, Eve, didn't venture far past the bar. The ones that I saw at the neighbors seemed nervous and on edge too.

Even Tootles, a normally docile, quiet dog, was now nothing more than a shivering heap in Cassie's lap. I usually tried to make a point of stopping to say hi to Cassie every morning before I had to do a few chores. She was a bright spot in my day. And here she was looking like a shell of her formal self, and she wore that same dingy swimsuit. She never was much for doing the laundry, but that suit could probably get up and tap dance at this point.

But this morning there was no Cassie sitting on the porch chair. It was empty, swinging itself in the breeze. It felt wrong and unnatural for her not to be sitting in it. I had to find out why.

I walked over to her house and knocked on the door. I peered through the screen and was anxious until I could hear Lyle shuffling his way to it.

"Well, hello there, girlie."

His voice was always so pleasant and gentle.

"Hey Lyle, where'd Cassie go? I didn't see her out in her chair today."

I felt like a busybody asking that.

"Well, we got a strange call last night."

"Oh?"

"Here, I'll let her tell ya."

Lyle looked perplexed, but just walked back toward the coffee pot and poured himself another cup. I could hear Cassie from her room.

"Who is that Lyle? Is that Brooke?"

Lyle rolled his eyes.

"Why don't you come over here and find out, woman."

He looked over at me and whispered, "She's been cuckoo ever since Ethel left. Can't wait till the woman gets back here."

Cassie came running in with more zip than she had shown for weeks. It was nice to see her wearing something different.

"SHE'S ALIVE!!! It's Ethel!!! She called me last night. She's here! She's back in Neelsville."

It was almost frightening watching Cassie jump and down, like a spoiled child who had just gotten her way. I had such different feelings about it. Like overwhelming dread. The feeling came at me in several waves, like it always did. And I almost felt like I couldn't move.

Oh No.

"She's alive?" I asked.

"Oh yes doll, very much so. Although, I need to give her a good clunk on the head for not telling any of us about it."

"Not telling us what?"

"Well, I guess she had worked herself into a tizzy a few weeks ago. Poor thing got it in her head that she never sees enough of her family. So, she decided that she would go on a little road trip to Arkansas. I do recall her saying that it had been awhile since she saw some kin. But can you imagine that, that pathetic creature driving through all that traffic? I mean she gets heart palpations just trying to merge."

I was hoping Cassie would get to the point.

"A little visit?"

"Yeah, she just wanted to visit some family. I wished she would have spoken to me about it beforehand; I would have loved to have gone with her. I haven't been on a good ole fashioned road trip in ages. Say, Lyles, why is it that we can't seem to do that?"

I gave Cassie a look of frustration.

"Oh yes, back to the point. Umm, well she's here, and I am beyond grateful."

"But doesn't that seem odd, Cassie? Doesn't she usually tell you everything?"

Cassie took out a cigarette and lit it showing her long nails. They were painted in bubble-gum pink.

"Sometimes it's good for people to expand their horizons. You know what I mean, doll?"

I kind of let that sink in a moment while Cassie's exhaled smoke trailed throughout the room.

"And thank Christ, she's back."

Lyle had been leaning on the counter, drinking coffee and lost in thought. I was starting to get a read on what he was thinking, and it had nothing to do with Ethel.

"You know, I saw the weirdest thing this morning."

Cassie wasn't having any part of it.

"Lyle, we are TALKIN ABOUT ETHEL!"

He ignored her.

"Went out fishing, saw the biggest looking mud turtle I've ever seen in my life. I mean, this thing was prehistoric, HUGE. And its eyes, well, they weren't turtle eyes if you ask me."

Cassie stood there with her arm across herself, still with the lit cigarette. She looked like she wanted to put it out on Lyle. She looked like her firecracker was lit, and her mind was running the same.

"Oh dear Christ, Lyle, was the creamer in your coffee spoiled? What will it be next? Frogs that fly? Now enlighten me, please, what does a cotton pickin' turtle have to do with finding Ethel?"

Lyle was fixated on something he had seen. And it wasn't just the turtle. The way he was thinking was he thought this whole Ethel story was hokey.

"Just saying. Never saw turtles with eyes like that, as all."

Cassie rolled her eyes.

"You'd think he saw a dinosaur. You *do* know this lake has its share of snapping turtles. You've lived here all your life, I didn't know you had such an aversion to turtles."

Lyle was peeved.

"But I haven't seen anything like this one! You are always asking about my fishing trips, I tell you about it, and you rip me in two. And this Ethel thing, I'm telling you, it just isn't right!! She calls to tell you when she's taken a dump, and out of the blue she just gets up and leaves? I'm telling you; something just isn't right!"

I looked over at Lyle. Crap Lyle, don't say anything more. How did he notice??

"You didn't see how she looked at the picnic? Woman you must be damn near cross-eyed!!"

Hold it together Lyle. I couldn't have agreed more. Lyle wasn't buying the horse manure either. I felt bad for reading his mind, so I quick switched it off.

"Not all her oars were ever in the water anyway. No wonder you two get along so well."

Lyle walked back into the living room as he was doing the cuckoo sign with his hand. He found his easy chair and plopped down into it.

Cassie leaned in. "I swear he gets more and more cantankerous every day. Like a dog chewing after his own tail. He tries me silly sometimes!"

"You think everyone is crazy, Lyle. All that matters is, SHE'S OK. Oh, thank the lord in heaven, Ethel is ok."

"Yes, thank the lord!" Lyle yelled from the other room.

"Were all glad she's back too, Cassie. I'll make sure to pass this info along to my parents."

"That would be great doll, just a big misunderstanding is all."

It was hard to believe. Just last week the whole town was on fire about Ethel's whereabouts, even thinking she was murdered. And turns out, she was just visiting family. Could Aaron have been possibly wrong?

Who was I kidding?

"Did you talk with her long, Cassie? Is she coming here today?"

"Well, of course, she's coming to see me doll. She would never miss your parents' barbecue. She also mentioned that she was making something extra special for the occasion. A little something to make up for causing such a stir."

I bet she did.

"Thanks, Cass, I'll let my parents know.

I needed to find Aaron, and NOW.

I ran back to my house and looked for a sweatshirt. My heart raced so fast I thought it was going to beat out of my chest. I was going to have to find him out in the woods again. The last few days he was scouring over everything in the woods that could lead to any possible clues about any distractors in the area, and what might have happened to Ethel. He did this with the water to.

However, he didn't enter into the lake by our resort. It was too conspicuous. We decided it would be better if we walked down to the bridge. There was a place underneath the bridge that a few of us went just to sit and talk. It was deceiving because the water looked shallow and innocent here at the rocks, but very quickly there was a huge drop off point, and it ran deep.

I found out the hard way one day while swimming there. One minute I was walking in the mushy sand, the next I stepped one foot too far. Right under the bridge, there was nothing but a bunch of boulders to walk on. This is where I would sit and watch Aaron walk into the lake and go under. Right before he stepped in, he would turn around, make that dazzling grin of his, and tell me not to worry. Then he would just go under and not come up. And there I would sit, with my heart in my throat.

And worry is precisely what I did.

Sometimes he wouldn't come up for hours. And I just couldn't leave right away. Even though he assured me that he was very safe. I always liked to linger there for just a few minutes. Sometimes I would notice bubbles swell up to the surface of the lake. They might have been from him, maybe not.

I never really knew, and it was an unsettling thought. It made me think about how our lungs were different. He was different in so many ways. And he was more than equipped to being underwater for an unusually long time. It was a hard concept to grasp because he looked so human, he breathed liked us to. But he breathed *differently*, he told me.

He told me once he was underwater, he could get really far in a short amount of time. And that it would be much safer for me to get back home. He didn't like me to be alone even if the distractors were far away.

Sometimes I wondered if Marjorie saw us go down to the bridge. Her tavern was just a stone's throw away. I wonder what it would be like to live above a tavern, and she had done it most of her life. I can't imagine that you would get any decent amount of quiet.

I just hoped she hadn't seen Aaron and me. And if she did, she kept it to herself.

She Brought
Potato Salad

*T*ootles sat on Cassie's lap, shaking like a leaf, her eyes were wide and full of fright. She kept looking up every few minutes, and over at me to see if I had the answers.

I wish I did, you poor thing.

I understood her pain. I was more frightened than I had ever been, and I had no idea what to expect from Ethel. I half expected her to come back looking like she was dipped in a coating of evil. But I knew better. She wasn't going to let herself be seen like that.

"She's been like this all morning. Don't understand it."

Cassie gave her a little love squeeze and reassured her in the way that only she could.

"Oh my little bugle puppy, you will be fine, I promise."

Tootles wasn't buying it. But Cassie didn't notice, she was too excited to see her friend again. Cassie seemed back to her normal, colorful self. Lyle was in deep conversation beside her, talking about fish migration and turtles to one of our tenants at the resort.

I couldn't help but get a strong weariness from his mind that hadn't been there before. He was a lot more guarded now. And he was even questioning himself more. I was trying to figure out why that was. Maybe he was starting to see things, too. I felt bad for Lyle. He was one of the sanest people here. I wished I could tell him.

I skipped the brat bun and stabbed the last piece of a brat with my wimpy plastic fork, breaking it. My paper plate was ready for the trash can. I tried anything to get my mind off of what was lurking around us. Tootles and I were the only ones that were in on it. That and Penny, of course.

Penny.

What had happened to her? Mom said their family would be staying for three weeks. But every time I went to her cabin she was never home. It was always her dad that answered the door. *The preacher.* And whenever he did, he looked lost in thought, deep bags under his eyes.

It was like his whole family knew what was going on and he didn't want me talking to his daughter. I couldn't much blame him. I didn't know or understand exactly what was going on myself. Sometimes I would see Penny walking along the shore, staring out at the lake. But when I would come down to talk, she would always be gone.

I knew that I needed to start eating better. I needed every bit of nourishment because I needed to be strong as I possibly could. There was a great storm coming.

The puppy sensed something unsavory lurking about in the crowd. Everyone seemed happily oblivious. I wished Aaron could get here soon. I could feel that he was somewhere nearby.

What was weird was the trees around us seemed to sense this, as well too. I could almost feel them shivering in the warm summer breeze. It was an odd experience, but not unpleasant.

I looked up. The hues of the leaves looked a bit different. Like they were purple, and it wasn't anytime near fall.

The trees knew.

Ever since I saw the one come to life near Aaron, I could never think of trees in the same way again. I treated them like they were human, like each of them had their own souls. Seeing one come to life could do that to you. But I've always liked trees, so it wasn't much of a stretch to think of them that way.

I prayed Aaron could make it to the party. I couldn't shake off the prickly sensation that one of these things was already here. I glanced over toward the direction of the pool. Lots of people around now, and it was horribly humid. The ends of my hair liked clinging to my face.

Drawing in a good breath without feeling winded was hard. If it weren't for the nice breeze coming off the lake, it would have been unbearable to eat. I could hear people splashing and jumping in the pool, not a care in the world. And the sun seemed to emphasize the fact. The pool was a perfect shade of turquoise. My dad was happy for that, no doubt.

I gazed down over at the lake. Not many fishermen since fish never liked to feed when it was so hot. Next best chance would be this evening. There was still a few determined fishermen. I watched as someone on dock one casted out. He slowly trolled his bobber back, perfectly content. So far, nothing out of the ordinary here.

I laughed to myself thinking how he would react if he caught Aaron on his fishing line. He could be swimming about down there now for all I knew. The man would probably drop dead of a heart attack right there. But Aaron was nice to people. He genuinely cared about them. He would never willingly scare someone like that.

I looked around at the faceless, nameless people that had just checked in earlier today. Most were busy eating, or in casual conversation. Nothing looked evil, sinister, or out of place. The food was even perfect. Watermelon sat in a perfect little-repeated triangle wedges on the cutting board. Trays of pasta and potato salad sat, chilled and ready to eat. And another batch of brats was cooking up on the grill. Mom made sure of that. And things that haven't been touched had a thin layer of tin foil on it just to keep the bugs at bay.

That's what scared me the most, from the outside everything was looking hunky dory.

Just what a distractor would like.

I knew I would be seeing Ethel and I practiced as much as I could about how our meeting would go.

I even stood in front of the mirror and copied my mannerisms and smiled over and over to get it right:

"Well hi there, Ethel. How are you?"

Just be courteous, but not overly friendly.

"Oh, that's terrible."

"You had us so worried."

"How was the traffic?"

"I bet it was nice to see your family again."

"We are so glad you are ok."

"We missed having you here."

I tried to imagine Ethel now as a monster. I mean, I wasn't 100% sure of it, but Aaron was. I hoped I could just keep my cool around her. I was terrified of losing it right there. But I had to be strong. Our whole family and town pretty much depended on it.

I had to sound convincing when she told me about visiting her family. I just didn't quite know how I was going to pull off looking concerned. Lying was something I was never good at. Even little white ones, it was just how I was wired. I was afraid Ethel would pick up on that right away.

I had to make sure to ask her about her relatives. I could not mess that up. AT ALL.

Because if I did, it meant sure slaughter for our whole resort, maybe not that minute, or even that day. But it meant shortly. Heck, even the town. I had to do everything I could not to give anything away. Even if it was glaringly apparent that she was one of them. I just wish she would get here already. The thought of it almost made me more nervous.

"So, when is Ethel coming?" I tried hiding my high-pitched nervousness.

"She's just finishing up her special potato salad, doll. She'll be here. She's anxious to see ya all, too."

I bet it was special.

Lyle gave me a rather sorted look. I wondered if he wasn't on to all this crazy stuff. Ethel annoyed him to no end, and I'm sure she was the topic of many conversations in that household.

I nervously looked around the resort grounds. She would be driving in at any moment.

To keep my mind off things, I decided to go inside the house and see if mom needed any help with the food. I walked in and found her buzzing around in the kitchen, normal for mom. She was cutting up cake in neat, square-like pieces.

"Hey, honey! How's it going out there?"

Despite waiting for Ethel to come, it would have been an almost pleasant afternoon.

"Good so far. Everyone looks like their having fun."

"Good."

As I grabbed two plates of cake, I heard the sound of someone pulling into the drive.

The hairs on the back of my neck stood up. I carefully looked out the window. It was eerie knowing that whatever now inhabited Ethel was now clacking her heels up our paved driveway.

It was her. She was carrying a plate of food covered with tin foil.

I wouldn't eat that for a million bucks.

She had a huge printed scarf wrapped around her head like a turbin, and a big smile to go with it.

When she saw us, she waved.

Here we go.

"Hi, y'all, what's going on?"

It was Aaron. He had snuck up on me.

IT'S ABOUT FRICKIN' TIME.

I tried to sound as normal as possible.

"Thank God, you're here."

I was so relieved I wanted to cry.

"Sorry, unexpected delays."

I tried whispering under my breath.

"Ethel is here."

"I know."

"And um, there's something up with the trees."

"Trees have always been sensitive to us and our counterparts."

I watched Ethel with the fake smile that could have lit up a Christmas tree. She never looked more frightening.

I whispered in Aaron's ear.

"I don't think I can do this. Acting normal with all this going on."

"You just have to. Just follow my lead."

"Well, hello there, neighbors."

Ethel was going from person to person, hugging and smiling. Shaking her head, saying how everything got so blown out of proportion.

Cassie greeted her long-lost best friend with the biggest bear hug in the world. It went on for several uncomfortably long moments. Ethel gave her a few reassuring pats on her back.

"I just can't tell ya how glad I am that you're back. You had us all in such a fright, darling. Please don't do a stupid stunt like that ever again."

"Well, I won't, Ms. Cassie DuPree. My goodness, dear, you do get in such a dramatic state."

Ethel set down her salad at the picnic table, and mom came up behind her.

"We're so glad you're back Ethel. But don't do that to us again, please. We thought Cassie here was gonna have to be sedated."

"Oh no darling, never again."

Ethel stood up and hugged mom. I shivered. I didn't like that thing touching her. Not even in pretense.

"So, how have you all been?"

She looked in my direction. I froze for half a second. I could feel Aaron's reassuring touch on my knee.

"Doing good. How about you? I guess you sure scared everyone."

I really just needed to shut-up. I probably looked as convincing as an alligator.

"Oh, I know, it's just been so darn long since I've seen family you know. It's good to take advantage of every bit of time you've got."

"Where did you travel?" Aaron said.

While Aaron asked her questions, I tried reading a little bit of her mind. And as I suspected, it was a waste of time. It was locked up tighter than a drum. No amount of trying was going to get in there.

"Arkansas, that's where I'm from."

Aaron was testing out the waters. He knew very well what she was, but did the thing know about him or even me knowing?

"It's always fun on the road. Such beautiful countryside."

I saw Ethel eye Aaron strangely. And I wanted to be sick every time I looked at her. I couldn't help it.

"Where exactly are you from? Aaron, was it?"

"Chicago."

"Well then, what brings you up here?"

"Isn't it obvious? Unless you hate the woods, lake, and trees."

"You got that right. I don't know how anyone couldn't appreciate all this nature surrounding us."

Ethel wasn't missing a beat. And a few feet above our heads stood our hundred-year-old oak tree. Its thick trunk stood massive amongst all the other trees. It had frail, rail-like branches that were twisted up into a knotted mess above us, providing just the right shade. I couldn't help but watch that tree. And if I wasn't mistaken, it almost looked like it was shivering.

I looked around the group to see if I was the only one privy to this. No one else seemed to notice. Aaron must have heard my questions. He turned his head toward me and gently said,

"Yes."

So, he had turned his mind reading on, not that he had ever had it off. It was just startling sometimes for him to always know what I was thinking. But that was fine by me. The more he could find out about the thing that was in Ethel, the better.

Everyone seemed to have moved on from Ethel's blunt departure last week. It only caused a minor firestorm in Neelsville, people both in the town and surrounding it thought she was murdered. It was the biggest story around here. But now here she was again, right out of the blue, attending one of my parents' barbecues and everything was back to normal. But there was one other living thing that wasn't buying into this, and that was Tootles. I watched her all curled up in Cassie's lap, looking like she wanted to snap a finger off. She stared in Ethel's direction, a low growl caught in her throat.

I was seriously frightened for the dog.

Cassie was trying her best to calm her down, but it wasn't working.

"Well, I just declare, I don't remember Tootles behaving so crazy. What is wrong with you, girl?"

I had to admit; you couldn't blame the dog, I was shaking, too. And Aaron was doing a good job of keeping me calm by holding my hand underneath the table.

"I better bring this yappy thing home. I'll be right back."

"You've spoiled her rotten, that's what," Lyle said in between bites of baked beans.

I couldn't help but keep my eyes fixed on the monster that was now Ethel. She was sitting across from me. I tried watching her hands, her face, all of her movements. I tried to be casual about it, I didn't want her to think I was staring.

It was hard being this close to her. I watched as she took a spoonful of potato salad. One thing that I couldn't get past was the elasticity of her skin. It looked like it had a plastic component to it, and I couldn't believe that no one else could see this. To me, it looked creepy and stuck out like a sore thumb. To everyone else, I guess not so much.

I bet poor Tootles was probably relieved to be back at Cassie's cabin. I envied her.

"My, this potato salad is quite delicious."

What, you don't grow potatoes where you are from?

Aaron gave me a little warning look.

"Why thanks, Ethel. It's a favorite of mine, too." Margie said.

Margie didn't seem to notice anything different about Ethel, either. But then again, Margie was always the poker face.

I had to fight the urge not to knock these people in the head with a baseball bat. In their defense, Aaron did say things would be more clear to me than other people. Thank god Aaron was here or I would have lost my mind.

"Could you pass me the ketchup, dear?" Ethel said.

She was asking me a question. Try to be casual about it.

I guess monsters like ketchup.

I passed her the bottle, and our hands touched for a brief second. At that moment I could see a little recognition of something that crossed her eyes. But it was slight, and she recovered quickly.

They are very patient and very good at what they do. And they can adapt to any situation rather quickly.

I suddenly felt like I was out of breath. I bet she had me pegged already. I could feel anxiety creeping up my spine, and I felt the need to leave before it was too late. I turned to Aaron, and I could tell by the look on his face that he had heard our slight but important exchange. I just wondered what he was getting from her.

"I'm gonna go get some water."

I couldn't sit one more minute across from her anymore. I felt like I was having an allergic reaction. Probably from Ethel. As I quickly got up from the table, I could feel a subtle prickly sensation around the back of my neck. It felt the same as if my foot had fallen asleep, accept this was my neck. It felt like something was trying to will its way into my head, peering into my thoughts. It was very unsettling, and I was trying like crazy not to let in whatever it was.

Now the sensation was at my temples.

I knew it was Ethel. She was trying to force her way in, figure out what I knew. And I wasn't going to let her. The pain in my temple was worse now and pounding.

Whatever was left of Ethel is long gone now.

As soon as I stepped into the house, the pain was more like a dull roar.

Ok. Maybe her powers only worked in short range. This was good.

It was unnerving having that thing sitting there on the picnic table, amongst my family and friends, all the while I had to play like everything was perfectly normal.

I was done for the afternoon, I didn't want to be anywhere near the distractors. And I didn't want anybody I knew around them either. I went to the window and gently pulled the lace curtain back. I could see her through them, looking pleased as punch. I could see Aaron was discussing something with her, probably something mundane like the weather.

He could still listen in on what she was really thinking. I hoped he was getting as much information as he could. I guess monsters weren't impervious to charm. His back was to me, but he looked like he was fine, for now. I pulled the curtain back. I didn't want her seeing me. I had to trust him.

I sure hoped she wouldn't try anything.

I just wished that whatever was going to happen would do so already. I was tired of hiding. I looked out the window again and noticed Cassie had joined the group again, minus Tootles. She sat down next to her friend beaming from ear to ear.

How could Cassie overlook all the sudden changes in her friend? I could only hope that whatever was in Ethel would never get to anybody else at this resort. Or anybody in this town for that matter.

I poured myself a glass of water and let the coolness coat my throat. I poured myself another and drank that one down too. Aaron had walked in shortly after.

"She's one of them alright. She needs to be destroyed, as soon as possible. Tonight."

I felt sick.

"What was she thinking Aaron?"

"She's a little bit wary, which is good. She's not going to do anything while the party is still going on. But she's plotting something. One thing we got going for us is she doesn't suspect anything from me."

"That's strange because she was trying to get to me."

"I was afraid of that. Humans are easier to detect then us."

"Well, that's comforting."

"I felt her try, but I didn't let her in. When I came in here, the feeling stopped."

"Ok, good. Well, she must be a weaker species of distractor then. That's good to know."

"What do we do now?"

"I would like to get you and your family out of here as soon as possible. But I know it would cause a stir, and we risk attracting more of them here. We need to get this done, and it needs to be tonight. They have more of an edge at night. And I've already asked my brother to come. I think we're gonna need help with this one."

"Your brother? How long has he been here?"

Aaron stared at me.

"The less you know about him, the better."

He seemed suddenly annoyed.

"What do you mean?"

"Nothing. Just, well, I'll feel better once you meet him."

"Why, is he that bad?"

"No, and don't be scared. He won't ever hurt you."

"Ok I wasn't, but now that you said something about it, maybe I am a little."

"It's just he's so, unstoppable. And I wouldn't put it past him to try something on you. I didn't want to ask him to come here, but he knows how to fight."

"What? Try what on me exactly?"

"Well, with Marcus, he gets distracted, easily. With the female species, I mean. He has a good dose of what I guess you guys would call Testosterone."

"But I thought you guys were alien? Isn't that something reserved for humans?"

"Yes, but we also have our version:"

"Ok, well I'm sure it will be fine."

"Yes, probably will. But you've never met Marcus. I know what he is capable of. And, so does he. He doesn't make any apologies for it either. But, I honestly don't know of a better fighter than him. He's used to fighting these distractors."

Aaron just gave me a look.

"Then it will be fine."

"Yes, it will be fine."

Aaron kissed me on the forehead.

"He'll be here soon."

The party was winding down. I talked Patti and her friends into coming inside and watching a movie. Thank goodness that she just did it. I didn't want that thing looking at her.

Lyle and Cassie were still lingering over a few after dinner drinks. Ethel had left, thank goodness. Said she wanted to take a nap. I was so glad, and the trees were, too.

The leaves were now back to their beautiful summertime green. I was never so happy to see that color again. I was still astonished that no one else noticed this.

THE FIGHT

*M*arcus reminded me of a more dirtier, rugged version of Aaron. He was nice looking that was for sure; cut from the same cloth, but with rougher scissors. I couldn't take my eyes off the huge dagger that he had on his belt. And I couldn't read his mind, either. I wish I could have, everything about him said dangerous. The moon reflected off of him, and just emphasized the fact that he was huge, muscular, and no-nonsense.

They both decided the best way to take Ethel by surprise was by water. And we were going to take one of my dad's canoes to her house. We would have the advantage by entering from the lake. I don't know why they thought this, but I just went along with it. Apparently, Marcus had fought with them before.

Aaron wanted me close, he knew they may try to use me as leverage. And I was shaking with fright. In fact, it was hard sitting in the canoe with Marcus sitting so close. In the evening light, he looked a little like a monster himself.

I sat in the middle while Aaron and Marcus sat at either end, gently gliding the paddle in and out of the water. Neither had a shirt on, so I had a good view of Aaron's muscles every time he paddled the canoe. It reassured me somewhat, seeing the strength in his arms, but I was terrified. It was unsettling to have Marcus sitting behind me. I had no idea what he was thinking.

Ethel didn't live far down Pony road, so her house came into view way too soon for my liking. It was eerie sitting under the moon's glow, knowing all this strange stuff was about to come to a head.

They guided the canoe straight up to her dock, and they both slowly climbed out of it, and carefully into the water. The cool water temps didn't affect them at all.

Aaron turned his head toward me.

"Be careful. At this point, they like to disguise themselves. And they can do that with anything, any animal in the area."

"You mean like change into a rabbit or something?"

"I wouldn't put it past them," Marcus said.

"Quiet!" Aaron whispered.

Marcus watched the dark water intently. He was very much on edge.

"Whatever you do, Brooke, stay here in the canoe. We know she's in there, and we're going to get her."

As they paddled closer towards shore, I could now see Ethel's house. I couldn't help but wonder what she was doing.

Aaron looked over and whispered.

"This will take no time at all. Don't worry."

Yeah, don't worry. Cause going after monsters is a normal occurrence here.

"I won't let anything happen to you."

I'm glad he was so sure, because I sure wasn't.

I watched as they both slowly climbed out of the lake, and gingerly walked closer up to her property. Marcus took out his dagger. He looked like Hercules walking around on Ethel's freshly mowed lawn. She was sure on it when it came to small details. We were all out of the water, but I could hear it bubbling behind us.

"Aaron, she's manipulating the lake."

Marcus walked back to shore and put his hand to test it.

"It's boiling. Well, she knows were here."

"You had to have figured that, brother," Aaron said.

"Do not go in the water, whatever you do!" Aaron yelled.

"Doesn't that hurt?" I asked Marcus.

"The elements do not affect us."

"What do we do?"

"Follow me."

We made our way to her dock, and I ran to her boathouse. I stayed inside the door, so I could still see what was going on, and I watched Aaron and Marcus crouch down into her lawn. I looked up at the house and saw a figure at the window. It was Ethel alright. She quickly darted away from it, and what seemed just a few mere moments it looked like she had floated outside.

So much for outside appearances. I guess it wasn't needed anymore.

She was already coming toward us at the shore. What was scary was how she moved. Her body was floating just inches above the top of her lawn as she moved toward Marcus. It was a strange thing to see, and it petrified me. Her face took on a strange darkness that I've never seen before. I had to tell myself that she really wasn't Ethel anymore.

"Marcus!!"

That was the last thing Aaron said before Ethel jumped in the water, right for Marcus, grabbing his head and taking them both under.

"Stay here!!" Aaron yelled.

Aaron dove right in after them.

I watched nervously as I saw huge bubbles coming up to the surface.

"Aaron!!!"

I knew holding their breath was easy for them, but all I could think of was Aaron being stuck down in that water with Marcus, and Ethel holding them both down.

I was sick.

I walked down back to shore, looking for any signs of them, screaming Aaron's name.

I wanted to call the police, my parents, anybody.

What was taking them so long????

I tried willing Aaron and Marcus to come up. Seconds later, I saw Ethel shoot out from the water. Her eyes wide and big, looking around her as she crawled her way out.

I quickly recoiled in horror. I ducked down as soon as I could. And hoped like mad that she couldn't see me.

She didn't seem to notice, but she was running pretty fast, back toward her house. Good, she must have thought she was outnumbered.

She looked like a witch in her long, flowing dress.

Aaron finally brought his head up out of the water and jumped out and ran after her. She suddenly stopped and turned around.

She now looked exactly how she truly was: a dark, scary menace. Her face was evil. All pretend traces of Ethel were gone. That could be seen even in the dark.

"You'll never get all of us. You are already too late. We are already everywhere. And when our leader comes, you all will be finished. Doomed. And you."

To my horror, she was looking right in my direction.

"How does it feel to be inferior?"

And with that Ethel whipped up a round fireball out of nowhere and aimed it square at my head. I ducked down in time to see if fly over and land in the lake. It made a small hiss as the fire quickly died out.

"I really don't have a tolerance for you anymore," Aaron said.

Aaron leaped on her like a cougar. His strong, powerful hands were at her neck. But this thing was fast, and she rolled him off her back with ease. She was quite STRONG. Aaron got back up and ran after her.

Marcus finally came up out of the water then and hooked his spear to the bow. He quickly aimed one right in her direction. I watched as it flew through the air and straight into her chest. She looked down and seemed shocked at the sight of it. Like she couldn't believe what just happened. She lingered there for a moment, trying hard to pry it from her chest, but it wouldn't budge. She just stood there, impaled.

She let out the shrillest scream. Her grayish, long nails clawing and yanking at the spear, trying to get it out. But it was no use. Ethel never had long nails when she was human.

The thought made me sad, and I had to look away.

Her moment of frustration was long enough for Aaron to get on top of her. He brought out a shiny silver medallion from his pocket and laid it on her forehead.

Her face started steaming as she screamed. Her long limbs were trying to scratch at him from every direction. He was fast, though, ducking away just in time past her hands. She looked like she was having a seizure.

"NOOOOoooooo."

The medallion seemed to be dooming her more than the spear did. I watched in horror as what was left of Ethel finally take another breath.

Now she was just a deflated version of herself, lying in a dark heap in the grass. As soon as Aaron thought she was dead, he got up off her and walked towards me.

"You ok?"

"I think so."

Aaron had a match and quickly lit it and set her on fire. We watched as the flames reached high around us, then settled back on down. I watched as what was left of Ethel burn to ash. Charred pieces of her whirled about in the air.

"A distractor bitch bonfire," said Marcus.

I looked around for a minute and felt a bit of relief. I let it wash over me, and then did something I wanted to do for a long time; and that was cry.

The tears came rolling down and they didn't stop. Aaron took me in his arms and held me there for a while. I could have stayed cradled there for hours, except my parents were expecting me back home. However, it felt good to be there in his arms, hearing his heartbeat against his chest.

It still felt strange to think Aaron was an alien because he was looking more and more human to me every day.

Marcus came walking up.

Aaron took my hands and helped me up back on my feet.

"You did good, brother. And I don't believe we were properly introduced."

"Brooke, this is Marcus."

He extended his hand, and I shook it. His grip was confident, strong.

I tried wiping away tears as I tried to muster up a smile. But it was no use, I was a mess.

"Hello, Brooke. I'm afraid your charms have quite occupied my brother, in more ways than one."

"Well, I don't know what I do to him."

"Well, whatever it is, it suits him."

It was nice getting a compliment from Marcus. I felt like he wasn't someone that was very frivolous with words. If he said them, he meant it.

I smiled.

"You will have to come see our planet. It may help you understand some of the things we can do."

"Yeah, someday. I would like that."

"I can't stay brother; you know that."

"I know. Thanks, Marcus. I don't know if I could have done this one alone."

"Probably not. I mean it, Brooke, let Aaron take you to our lands."

"I will."

Marcus shook Aaron's hand. They said a few words I couldn't hear. Then Marcus ran back in the direction of the woods.

"Is that how he got here?"

"Something like that."

"Why is he leaving so soon?"

"Temptations."

"Oh. Do I wanna know?"

"Not tonight. That's for another time."

"Are you ever gonna show me what you use to get back and forth from your planet to ours?"

"Yes. But for now, let's get you back home in one piece, shall we? I think you've had quite enough adventure for one evening."

"I'm not that fragile you know."

He smiled and took my hand in his. Being in the presence of both Marcus and him made me feel quite small in comparison.

They were killers, that was obvious. And the way Marcus moved well, he looked like he'd done that a few times before. But I never felt so safe and loved then when I was by Aaron's side. He squeezed my hand again and gave me a small kiss on the cheek. I felt that electric spark between us again. But he had promised me that was as far as he would take it, for now.

"How are we going to explain this one?"

"We're not. Unfortunately, people disappear all the time. And she'll be on the back of a milk carton or a missing person list."

"How do you know about milk cartons?"

He grinned one of his gorgeous smiles of his.

"I know a little something about the human race. I've had to adapt after all."

I still had endless questions for him, but that, too, was for another day.

I couldn't help but feel bad about the real Ethel. She didn't deserve this.

"Where do you think she is now?"

Aaron smiled.

"Ethel the human is in a much better place. The distractor, however, is of no more."

"Cassie's gonna have a freakout."

"Well, she has Lyle, and she has her dog. And she has all of you."

"Yeah, but it's still gonna be hard on her."

The summertime flowers in the evening were fragrant in the air. The stars were out and twinkling, and it was a comfort to see them. At least they haven't gotten to the sky, yet.

I noticed that alongside the road, there were silvery patches of grey on the ground, catching the moonlight. I had never noticed that before. My heart sank.

"It's getting worse."

He cupped my face with his hands and looked deep into my eyes.

"We're gonna figure this thing out together, I promise. You won't be alone."

"But it's getting everywhere."

"I'm not going to let them. Believe me, we will defeat them Brooke."

"Ok." I believed him.

I didn't know what the future would hold, or what sort of odd fate awaited me. But for now, I just concentrated on his very capable, strong hand in mine. And how nice it felt to walk alone with him. Despite all the odds, we had managed to find each other, and that in itself was remarkable. We continued our walk down Pony Road, hand in hand back towards the resort. He assured me that for now, the distractors were far away. And for now I felt safe, and that was enough.

ACKNOWLEDGEMENTS

Having this book in your hands is nothing short of a miracle. Many burned dinners, a cluttered house, and disorganization was because of my writing, and to my family I am sorry for that. Thank you to my husband for his patience and encouragement on a daily basis with my writing, and believing in me. I've had ideas for this book for several years, but just didn't have the wherewithal or knowledge of what to do with it. I would like to thank Laura Eckert for her expertise, knowledge, and talent in the writing and publishing arena. Also, for pointing me in the right direction when it comes to publishing, and the confidence to go for it. I would like to thank Michelle Goraj for being one of the first people to say it was good enough to publish. Thank you to Erika Van Singel for wanting to expand on the character of Marcus. Thank you to Rochelle Dozeman for your constant encouragement, you are truly the light. ☺ Thank you to Allison Lynema for your enthusiasm in wanting to see my book in print. Thank you Mr. Zielinski for specific style changes, and overall just great pieces of information that helped give the book legs. Thank you to my parents for giving me such great memories of our little resort on a lake. Thank you to my sister for recommending a book to me that changed my life. A book that was a fun little side step away from endless hours of feedings, diaper changes, and sleep deprivation. Those unforgettable characters helped propel me to start reading and writing again. Thank you to Stephanie Meyer for Twilight. And for giving me the courage to go through with my book.